Watch for More Indigo Sea Press
Novels by Rachael Stratford

indigoseapress.com

# Right of Trespass

## By

## Rachael Stratford

Perseverance Books
Published by Indigo Sea Press
Winston-Salem

Perseverance Books
Indigo Sea Press
302 Ricks Drive
Winston-Salem, NC 27103

First Perseverance Books edition published January, 2016
Perseverance Books, Moon Sailor and all production design are trademarks of Indigo Sea Press, used under license.

For information regarding bulk purchases of this book, digital purchase and special discounts, please contact the publisher at indigoseapress.com

Cover design by Lazarus Barnhill

Manufactured in the United States of America
ISBN 978-1-63066-325-4

To my inspiration with heartfelt gratitude for
your presence in my life that gives
me an unexpected new beginning.

# Chapter One

Ellen woke, disturbed; something was not right. She lay very still, listening. It seemed a clap of thunder had boomed through her head. Had she been dreaming? Had something fallen? She could hear nothing out of the ordinary and rolled over to look at the clock. Seven in the morning. She had deliberately not set the alarm so she could sleep in this Saturday and not get up until she felt rested. What was it that had so abruptly jarred her awake? Her mind cast about trying to determine the cause, trying to quiet the niggling uneasiness, not yet realizing her apprehension would grow throughout the day.

She tried to remember if she had turned off the water in the greenhouses, closed down the windows and covered the outside plants. Sometimes she did wake with a pressing anxiety if she had left some chore undone. But she could think of nothing she had neglected to do. She smiled. Perhaps her psyche was alarmed that she had overslept. Within the past few weeks, Ellen had started enough plants to fully sustain her spring sales. Surely she could now allow a few days of relaxation.

She was so glad Bud had decided to join her in her now thriving business. Her nursery-cattle ranching enterprise required a considerable amount of effort to keep things running smoothly. And her brother needed some new occupation that would allow him to be his own boss, to make more of his own decisions. This seemed the perfect solution, as they both loved planting and growing things.

As she got up and reached for a pair of faded blue jeans, a black SUV roared down the gravel road in front

1

of her house. "Good Lord," she said aloud. *No one drives that fast out here in the country. What was after him?* she wondered. She pulled on a bright red sweatshirt, appreciating the warmth of it. It was chilly in her bedroom. Since it was the first day of April in Oklahoma, she could expect frost to crystallize the landscape for three more weeks or until approximately April 20th. Sitting on the edge of her bed, she pulled on western suede boots, the ones she loved the best. The suede was soft, and boots always fit better than shoes. Plus, the tough soles gave her a much heftier kick if she needed to force a drag pin or some such thing while hooking up the equipment. But the best part was never having to polish them.

After weaving her long, dark hair into one abundantly thick braid, beginning high on the back of her head, she turned and headed for the kitchen. Just then another vehicle, a burgundy Ford pick-up, flew hell-bent for leather past her house. Ellen thought she recognized the truck. It belonged to the new neighbor who had just purchased the 200-acre ranch adjoining her property on the east. The stirrings of agitation she had felt earlier returned.

*Not the way to start a good neighborly relationship,* she thought. *Hope that goose and his friends don't make a habit of driving like idiots. Jeez...do they think this is the Indianapolis Speedway?*

Ellen started the coffee. Then flipped on the TV, as she passed it on her way to the floor-to-ceiling windows in the den to check out the morning. The sun sent shafts of glittering light through the haze of fog still hanging in the tops of the trees. There was already a greening of grass in the pecan orchard between the house and road. Crocus blossoms of white, purple and porcelain blue lined the walk, and bright yellow daffodils formed a huge, solid ring in the center of the circular drive.

Everything seemed to be at peace. Even Miss Muffy, her favorite cat, sat calmly on the white board fence with her tail curled around in front of her feet, looking for the world like a beautiful, calico ampersand.

With a deep sigh, Ellen reflected on how much she loved her home in the country. The quiet tranquility sustained her soul. The chirping of the birds, the croaking of the frogs, the yapping of the coyote at night were all a part of the whole, yet were independent and free to do their own thing. The harmony of all she had found here reminded her that God's true promise must first be found inside one's self, independent of and not through anything or anyone else. She had struggled several years, working many overtime hours, scrimping and saving to insure that her then-husband could attain two college degrees. Her understanding was that when he had his degrees, he would work, pay the bills and help some with the domestic duties so she could also earn a degree. Instead, he broke her heart. After seven years of dutifully and laboriously fulfilling her end of the bargain, she had nothing but an aching emptiness, painful memories and no money.

Her mind turned away from the bitter past and focused hopefully on the sweeter promise of the present. The delicious aroma of coffee filled the room and teased the hunger that pushed itself into her awareness. She would call Bud and offer him breakfast: bacon and eggs with steaming biscuits and a thick, creamy, bacon-flavored gravy—even some wild plum jelly he loved so much. He could be there before breakfast was ready, since he lived only a short distance down the road. Jennifer, his significant other, had flown to Houston to be with her mother, who was having knee surgery. Bud was no prize cook himself, but loved a good meal, so he would appreciate the offer.

She picked up the phone, pushed the "A" button and

listened to the ringing. Out of the corner of her eye she spied her yellow tomcat, Old Yowler, creeping stealthily upon a chaparral. Frantically, she rapped knuckles against the glass to frighten away the bird lest he become only a pile of feathered remnants. Ellen prized the roadrunners, who were great snake catchers. She had far too many rattlers and water moccasins down by the creek. The bird took several flying leaps and was gone, his long tail causing him to teeter awkwardly as he paused momentarily on the fence.

Ellen cradled the phone, pushing aside the discomfort she felt when there was no answer.

Sliding open the glass door at the persistent yowling of her only male cat, she said, "I really named you right, didn't I, old fella? Seems pretty bad to me that the only guest I can entice for breakfast is a yowling nuisance."

She was gratified that he instantly stopped his awful noise and trotted into the house, stopping to rub up against her legs, thanking her in advance for the food he knew would be waiting.

Later in the day, feeling restless and needing to get something accomplished, Ellen decided to load Big John, the Limousin bull she had rented to father her new calf crop. Since he had fulfilled his duties and all her cows were now expectant mothers, she would return him to his owner.

*Why pay for feed and services no longer needed?* Ellen had to be frugal.

It had always been a challenge to figure out how to manage things alone, chores that really required at least two people. However, with determination and thoughtful persistence, Ellen had learned to be resourceful and tried to figure out in advance how to use the nature of the animals to help her achieve her goals. Many of her friends told her she was ridiculous

4

to mess with raising cattle in addition to her nursery business. But tending the cattle, watching them grow and get fat and naming almost every one of them, was a work of joy for her. She especially loved it when the new babies came.

*Maybe I just need babies of my own. Not likely. Not now that I'm...uh...spouseless,* she thought.

For several days Ellen had been feeding Big John in the trailer, starting out at the tailgate and moving the firm, tasty cubes further into the trailer with each meal. She thought today she could get him fully up into the trailer and slam the door before he realized what was going on. It was a daunting task she was never quite sure she could accomplish.

*Oh well, the best-laid plans of mice and men...and even women....*

Ellen called Bud again to see if she might be able to enlist his aid. After receiving no answer, she reluctantly hung up the phone and went to the crib to get a bucket of cubes.

Big John heard the clang of the gate and knew it was feeding time. He came on the run. It was always a fearful sight to see the 2000-pound creature running straight at her. Ellen couldn't force herself to stand until he reached her. He might not be able to stop soon enough. She hurriedly carried the bucket of cubes behind the trailer. Big John was not to be fooled. He was there in an instant, butting the bucket, demanding cubes. Ellen quickly opened the truck door and jumped inside the truck. She slid across the seat to get out the other side, spilling a few cubes as she went. Big John had practiced the procedure. He was at the other door before she could open it. She hesitated, trying to decide how to outsmart this big dude, for there was no question which one of them would win a pushing contest.

5

Finally, Ellen scooped up cubes and dumped them out the window. Big John came around the truck and was greedily chomping several at a time. Ellen knew she had only a few minutes to get the rest of them up in the trailer and to get out before Big John had finished his appetizer. She hurriedly jumped out the other door of the truck and ran to the back of the trailer. Taking a step up into it, she threw the cubes as far to the front as she could, trying to keep them in as neat a pile as possible. Big John was there as soon as she had stepped out of the trailer; thinking the cubes were still in the bucket, he was butting and pushing Ellen backwards. She set the bucket down and stepped away so he could check it out. Big John smelled the bucket and then started sniffing the ground. Some cubes had fallen close to the tailgate. He ate them, then proceeded to sniff his way up into the trailer. Soon he was totally in it. Ellen managed to slam and lock the gate behind him. With a sigh of relief, she thanked God and once again made a mental note that she should trade her trailer for one with no enclosing bars on the top. She might someday get trapped in there with no way out.

Ellen delivered Big John back to his owner. She was relieved the deed was done. Maybe in the future, Bud would be there to help her with this kind of work. Thinking of Bud, she decided to stop by his house to see if he had returned and to ask where he had been all day. She parked her truck and trailer along the side of the road and walked up the driveway to his house. Bud's yard was not large and did not accommodate backing and turning a trailer and, admittedly, she was still not a pro at it.

*Oh, good! He's here,* she reasoned as she saw Bud's tan Silverado parked in the driveway next to his cinnamon colored Camaro.

Ellen knocked and waited. There was no answer.

She knocked again and walked to the end of the porch to wait. She noticed deep, furrowed ruts leading out of the drive where someone had spun dirt and gravel while leaving in a hurry. She supposed Lila, his "ex," had come over to rub more salt into the wounds she had so cruelly dealt him. She must have left in a great tiff to have thrown that much dirt. Bud still had not answered the door. Ellen was turning to leave when she noticed a dark stain on the porch. Was that blood? There was more on the door jamb. The apprehension she felt in the morning returned, greatly amplified.

She knocked again and called loudly, "Bud! Bud, are you here? Are you okay?" There was no answer. She tried the door. It swung open. Chairs were overturned; some were broken. Shattered glass was on the floor and on the kitchen cabinet. There was a large pool of what appeared to be blood on the floor between the table and kitchen sink. Smaller splotches and splatters trailed across the floor to the door. A stained kitchen towel lay on the table, along with several pieces of paper, some of which had fallen to the floor. She felt her knees giving way beneath her and clutched the table for support. Confused and fearful, her mind frantically searched for answers. Who had done this and why?

Ellen pulled herself together enough to call the sheriff. With some difficulty, she conveyed the necessary information and location to the dispatcher. The sheriff, she was told, was on his way.

Upon his arrival, the sheriff introduced himself. With a precursory handshake that was damp, but firm, he said, "I'm David Hewitt, Hawkins County Sheriff."

He was a man of average height, who had begun to spread a little in the middle. His uniform fit snugly across shoulders that were beginning to stoop. Above a neat, but somewhat thick mustache, his eyes intently appraised her. His demeanor was almost unfriendly.

Ellen folded her arms in front of herself. She would have to pull her emotions together and be concise in reporting everything she knew about what had happened. And she realized she knew almost nothing.

Several uniformed deputies and other law enforcement officials arrived in different vehicles. Most of them ignored her or gave her only a slight nod.

One, however, did smile at her and said, "Hi." His eyes even crinkled. "Brady" was printed on the nametag above his pocket.

All of them immediately began to take pictures, measure tracks, study all aspects of the surroundings and put up yellow tape, slowly working their way into the house.

Sheriff Hewitt, however, leaned against the fender of his car and began to question Ellen.

"So you are Bud's sister?" he asked.

"Oh, you know my brother!" Ellen was surprised.

"We had met a few times, but I didn't really know him. When was the last time you saw him or talked to him?"

"Late yesterday about 6 p.m., I guess. We talked on the phone."

"Did he seem troubled about anything?"

"No. He was just anxious for Jennifer to come home," she replied.

Sheriff Hewitt pulled a rather small pipe from his breast pocket and tapped the bowl of it against his left palm. Putting it in his mouth without filling it, he puffed small whiffs of air, but mostly seemed to enjoy it as something to clamp his teeth onto.

"Who's Jennifer and why was she gone?"

"Jennifer is his fiancée. She's in Houston while her mother is having knee surgery."

After approximately twenty minutes of questioning, Ellen was finally able to volunteer the information about the two vehicles roaring down the road earlier.

"I don't know if this has anything to do with what happened here, but a black SUV came barreling down the road this morning; then close on his tail was a burgundy Ford truck. Since both were speeding and within minutes of each other, I thought they must…uh…well…uh… be connected somehow," Ellen offered. "I believe the burgundy truck belongs to my new neighbor."

She admitted that, of course, she had no way of knowing if there were any connections between the vehicles and what had happened to her brother and his house. Though she hesitated to call it an abduction, that's what it surely was. Bud would have called her if he had been able to use the phone.

The sheriff and his deputies finished their inspection and had fully taped off the area. Ellen still felt she could not leave. There were so many questions and no answers. But there was nothing here she could do. She drove home. Not bothering to unhitch, she went into the house. Though she didn't want to, she had to call Jennifer.

When they were first introduced, Ellen had liked Jennifer a lot and thought Jennifer and Bud were a perfect match. She often secretly wished Bud had met Jennifer first and married her instead of Lila. Since the divorce was never finalized, according to Lila, Jennifer and Bud would now have to wait to marry.

Nervously tapping her fingers on the desktop, Ellen counted the rings before Jennifer answered.

"Hi Jen, How are ya?"

"Hey, Ell! I'm good. How about you?"

"Not so good really. I'm afraid I have some bad news."

"What happened?" Ellen heard the tightening in her voice. "Is it Bud?"

"Yeah, Jen. He's not here. We don't know where he is. And the house has been trashed."

"Maybe he just went to see Perry to play poker with his friends and someone broke in."

"We don't know what happened, Jen. There's a lot of broken stuff and a good amount of blood on the floor and some outside. Of course, we don't know yet whose blood it is."

"Oh my God, Ell. Don't tell me he could be hurt."

"We really don't know anything yet."

"I'll catch the first flight back as soon as I can get a health care worker to look after mom. I'll call with my flight number and arrival time as soon as I book," she said.

Ellen hung up, glad Jen would be coming back soon. It would be good to have someone to talk to. But right now she would have to settle for a long walk.

Grabbing a light jacket against the late afternoon chill, Ellen did as she so often did when something bothered her. She trudged slowly down the path to the creek that crossed the back of her property, completely oblivious to all about her: the tall pecan trees, the showy-pink, peach blossoms, even the rows of onions and potatoes in the garden—all the things she had so enjoyed caring for. Seizer, her German Shepherd, trailed at a respectable distance, as if he knew she wanted no companion.

Baby, the little calf whose mother had died, came running up for her bottle even though it was not time for her dinner. Ellen gently rubbed her nose and walked on. Baby followed and bawled a few short, resentful objections, before giving up and going reluctantly back to the herd.

Ellen wandered on until she came to the edge of Sediment Creek that marked the boundary of her land. The water was clear and flowing, but not deep. It was usually comforting, quiet and relaxing just to sit and watch it flow through the meadow. She turned aside and found a small bank where she sank down on a sandy ledge, sheltered from the wind. She felt lost and alone. Bud was her last close relative. While she prayed that nothing bad had happened to him, deep within she knew better. There had been evidence of extreme trauma. Was all that blood his—or just partly his? Had he been able to deliver a few blows of his own? How could she find him? Help him? How did he leave—or who took him? Where was he?

Bud had always been a favorite person in her life. She had no other siblings. Her parents had been killed in an F4 tornado almost two years ago. She had to find Bud. Where to start? She had no clue.

As she sat there, letting the tears flow while the past claimed her thoughts, she gave in to memories of events that shaped the relationship she had with her missing brother.

In spite of her misery, she chuckled as she recalled his adventurous nature as a child, his uncanny ability to locate her most secret hiding places and steal her preciously rationed candy or gum. She remembered the time he drowned her baby chick after convincing her he could teach it to swim like a duck. Once he even took her lunch money to treat a friend to a milkshake. He had been a gregarious youngster, enjoying life and wanting everyone else to enjoy it as well. He also had a responsible side and had proven it more than once. He was only six years old when he first bravely assumed heroic responsibility.

Ellen vividly remembered feeling cold that morning, a few days after Easter Sunday. The day was clear and bright. There were beautiful yellow daffodils and red tulips along the lane that ran behind their house, all the way from the barn to the road. The wonderful smell of hickory smoke wafted out from under a black kettle filled with water her mother was heating to scrub the back porch.

It seemed incredible to Ellen that she could still feel that morning so intensely since she, herself, could have been no more than four years old. She and Bud each had a fluffy, yellow duck and Bud had talked her into "racing" them.

He wanted, as he had said, "To see which one can really stratch drabel." *Stratch drabel* meant to scratch gravel or to really be able to make the pebbles fly.

Ellen smiled as she recalled how they had argued when Bud insisted his duck should get a head start since it was probably a little smaller than hers. Mostly, she had listened as he told her just how he was going to conduct the race between two unwilling ducks. Where the finish line was to be and just what would happen if one duck got confused and went the wrong direction or stopped to peck and dawdle away his time. She could still see his exasperation as he put his hands on his hips and continued to enlighten her on the rules of the race.

Quite unexpectedly, his demeanor changed. He sucked in his breath. His eyes, bulging, were fixed on something fearful behind Ellen. Ducks forgotten, Bud yelled, "C'mon. There he is!" He started running towards the house.

Ellen had turned to see what had scared him so. At first she saw nothing, but had started towards the house, still looking back.

Bud looked back and screamed, "C'mon. It's that old mad dog."

Then Ellen saw the huge, yellow creature watching them as a cat watches a mouse. She started to whimper and run, but her feet got tangled up and she fell. Bud stopped and came back for her. She felt his anger.

His face was red as he yelled, "You better c'mon.

He's gonna git you." He grabbed her hand and jerked her up.

Ellen couldn't seem to keep from looking back and fell again.

Bud was frantic. He kept screaming, "Hurry, Hurry....he's gonna eat us up. C'mon... C'mon."

Ellen tried to do as he demanded, but she just couldn't seem to hurry fast enough.

Bud knew what he had to do. He didn't ask her to get up any more. He just started running, holding onto her hand, dragging her like a rag doll. Ellen could still taste the grit and smell the dirt he kicked into her face as he ran. She remembered how it felt to bump along the ground and how she had cried when he dragged her up the rough wooden steps skinning her knees and ripping her dress.

Ellen could almost feel the breath of the dog and could still hear the shrillness of Bud's frantic cries of "Mama, mama" as he neared the kitchen door.

Their mother saw them coming and flung open the door just in time for Bud to literally throw Ellen across the floor. She then slammed shut the heavy wooden door scant seconds before the angry, yellow monster hit the barriers and tore a hole in the screen. The dog went from open window to open window, jumping up against the weak, worn screens, determined to gain entrance to the house.

Their mother put Bud and Ellen in the middle of the bed while she found and loaded their father's .22 rifle. Bud didn't stay on the bed. He shadowed their mother as she followed the dog back and forth until she finally got good aim. Turning her head, she pulled the trigger. The bullet found its mark. The dog was hit but was able to run away.

Their father found the dog, dead, behind the barn

when he returned home late that afternoon. He recognized the dog. So they all loaded up in the old Chevy truck and went to tell Mr. Abernathy their mom had shot his dog.

Mr. Abernathy said old Ringo had recently been acting strange and had even tried to bite *him*. There had been reports of rabies in the county, so he was worried when the dog disappeared and wasn't sure what to do.

"It was the onliest thang a body could do wuz ta go ahead and shoot that dog," he told their mom. She felt better about shooting Mr. Abernathy's dog after that.

The excitement of the episode lasted for some time. Bud liked to tell everyone about the incident. He was very proud of their mom and bragged about her aim. As he poked his finger through the hole in the screen made by the single rifle shot, he would say, "Boy, just one shot. Pow! Right through that hole," as though the hole had been there first.

Ellen was sure Bud had never considered himself brave, never even thought he had saved her life. For though he bragged of his mother's great deed, he never once mentioned how he had gone back and dragged his baby sister to safety. But she would always remember the terror in his eyes, the flush on his cheeks and his shortness of breath as he, a six-year-old, struggled to fulfill a man-sized responsibility.

Tears still dampened Ellen's cheeks as the sun began to set. She rose to attend to her chores. A great emptiness overwhelmed her, and all seemed as dark as the approaching night.

She spoke softly as she left the banks of the stream. "My sweet brother, you were truly heroic, and I shall find you or never know peace again."

But how? Where to start? Perhaps the new neighbor with the burgundy truck would shed light on the problem.

# Chapter 2

"Is it okay if I scrub up Bud's house?" Ellen asked when she got Sheriff Hewitt on the phone the next morning. She didn't want Jennifer to see the unsettled condition of it, especially the kitchen Jennifer had so carefully remodeled and been so pleased with. But mostly she wanted to remove all the bloodstains that signified someone had been terribly injured.

"Sure is. We're finished with our investigation there. The yellow tape should be down within the hour."

While she had him on the phone, Ellen tried to find out if they had turned up any evidence.

"Not really much to go on." he said. "Someone sure made a mess and left in a hurry. We don't have the results of the forensics yet, of course."

Ellen felt a jolt of anger. His attitude seemed far too casual—too indifferent. Didn't he realize her brother could be in the hands of criminals or dying somewhere? After all the questions he had asked her about possibilities and probabilities on the day of the crime, had he not discovered any clues at all to indicate a motive? Had he a suspect, a direction in which to start probing, kicking butt or at least shaking the bushes?

"Were you able to get any information from the neighbor? Was he the man in the burgundy truck that morning and did he see anything? Did he see the black SUV and did he know them?" Ellen realized she was quizzing the sheriff somewhat more forcefully than was appropriate.

"Yes," replied Sheriff Hewitt, seemingly unperturbed by Ellen's demands. "He's quite a nice fellow, isn't he?"

"I don't know. I've not met him."

"Well, I think he'll make you a mighty fine neighbor," drawled the sheriff. "And yes, he did drive down the road out there that morning about the same time you indicated, but doesn't think he was speeding. Didn't recall seeing a black SUV."

"Well, he must be blind, as well as unable to read speedometers," Ellen snapped.

"Whoa girl, let's get a few more facts together, and then we'll know where the blame lies," cautioned the sheriff. "I know you're frantic to locate your brother and so are we, but some things take time. I will let you know when we get a real solid lead."

Ellen realized the sheriff had no obligation to keep her informed of every detail in the investigation, and she could not afford to alienate him. She needed him in her corner.

Thanking him, she hung up reluctantly, thinking maybe she might just have to meet that "mighty fine neighbor" herself. And maybe he would be more candid with her than with an officer of the law...but then maybe not.

Jennifer returned from Houston the following day. Ellen drove to Will Rogers Airport in Oklahoma City to pick her up. She pulled up to the curb just as Jennifer exited the terminal. She helped get Jennifer's bags in the hatchback of her used, but still serviceable beige Honda Odyssey. After they were buckled up and ready to roll, Ellen took a good look at Jennifer and noted how tired and frazzled she looked. Her blond, honey-colored hair was clasped in a ponytail. Several strands had escaped and stuck to her cheeks and the back of her neck. Her light blue eyes looked darker with eyeliner smudges underneath, and the corners of her mouth were turned down dejectedly.

"You really look ill. Are you okay?" queried Ellen.

"I'm beat. I'm relieved though that I found a great caregiver for mom, and she's recovering nicely. Is there any news at all about Bud since we talked?"

"None. I would have called you if there had been. The sheriff is waiting for forensic test results, like fingerprints and blood type, etc. He's moving awfully slow, it seems to me. I wish he seemed more determined or worried or something. He just seems to...well, to not be worried. Makes me want to do something on my own. I don't know what, but something, you know," answered Ellen.

"Yes, I'm sure there's only so much he can do, and I know he's not nearly as frantic as we are, and that's probably good. Cool head, you know. But I'm like you. How can we just do nothing and wait?" Jennifer asked.

"Yeah, Jen, and I think that guy next door is the first place to start. Sheriff Hewitt said he thought he would be a mighty fine neighbor. I'm not so sure." After a pause, Ellen offered, "Why don't you lean the seat back and try to sleep a little? It will be at least two hours before we're home. You look completely exhausted."

"Yeah, Ell, I am. And on top of it all, I have been queasy and nauseous ever since I left for Houston. It could be the trip and all the other stress, but Ell, I think I may be pregnant."

Before thinking, Ellen blurted out, "Oh, what a blessing. Bud will be so happy." She hesitated, remembering and then continued, "I know...timing and all that, but it's still a blessing."

"Yes, Bud and I want children, and soon, but we did so want to be married first, and this awful thing with Lila has really upset the applecart.

The sun was about to set as they reached Bud's empty house. Ellen helped Jennifer with her luggage. She was torn between the need to go home and wanting to stay with Jennifer to make sure she was going to be okay.

"Jen, why don't you spend the night with me—or even a few days—rather than being here alone?" she asked.

"I'm going to have to brave it alone sometime soon. I guess it might as well be now as later," answered Jennifer. "If it turns out to be too much, I'll call you. At least stay a bit and have tea with me, if you have time."

After putting on the kettle, Jennifer wanted to walk through the house, assessing the damage. Ellen accompanied her.

"I straightened things as much as possible. You'll notice some chairs, glasses and knick-knacks missing. I put the broken things out in the storage building behind the garage."

Jennifer reached for a tissue, wiped a tear from her cheek, and taking a deep breath, said, "Thanks, Ell, for clearing away all the broken pieces."

Then, wrapping her arms around herself as though she needed to be hugged, she started sobbing. "Oh God, where is he? What can we do to find him? I cannot bear it without him! Oh, Ell, what can we do?"

Tears were flowing down Ellen's own cheeks as she put her arms around Jennifer. "I don't know, but we will find him. We will look everywhere and never stop until we do."

Ellen hoped she didn't sound as hopeless as she felt. She had made several attempts to talk to the neighbor, but could never find him at home.

With her arms still around Jennifer, Ellen started moving toward the kitchen. "Let's have some tea, and maybe we can figure out where to start."

The tea was good and refreshing and gave Ellen an energy boost. *Maybe enough to get my chores done,* she thought.

Right of Trespass

As Jennifer gathered the glasses and set them in the sink, she reached for an object on the windowsill.

"Oh, Ell, is this yours?" She extended her hand, holding a beautiful circle of golden lace with what appeared to be a diamond in the center.

"No," answered Ellen, "I found it under the edge of the kitchen cabinet when I was cleaning. I thought it was yours. Looks expensive. What is it really?"

"Yeah, it does look expensive. Like the real stuff. I've never seen it before. It's not mine. I don't really know what it is. Could be broken off of an ear ring, a broach or even a button," replied Jennifer.

"It may be evidence the sheriff should have," said Ellen. "Hang on to it, and we will get it to him tomorrow."

Shortly, Ellen said her good-byes and walked to her car. Opening the door, she heard the purr of an engine and turned to see a red burgundy truck glide up beside her.

She could not discern a lot through tinted windows, but momentarily a white ball cap sporting the letters "USA" emerged, and beneath the bill of the cap was a pair of the bluest eyes Ellen had ever seen.

A flicker of a smile crossed his face before his countenance sobered. He exited his vehicle and approached Ellen as she closed her door and took a step toward him.

By all rational assessment, it was a most bizarre premonition. Yet, it was the most positive statement ever made by her inner self. She was at first taken by surprise, which gave way to awareness of having ended a life-long search. This was quickly replaced by anger and finally fear as Ellen sensed, in the flash of a moment, that her direction in life was suddenly changed and irrevocably linked, somehow, to this dark-haired stranger and ultimate danger.

19

He started to speak; then as his eyes met hers, he hesitated. Was he experiencing the warning she felt?

"I'm Zack Cunningham, your new neighbor from down the road. Would you be Jennifer Phillips?" he asked.

*Asked rather stiffly*, Ellen thought.

"No, I'm Ellen Wade. Jennifer is inside," replied Ellen as she started walking toward the house. She was not leaving yet, no matter what. Here was an opportunity to maybe find out if this guy knew anything about her brother and his disappearance. And perhaps decide why he had caused such a strange upheaval of her emotions.

Ellen tapped lightly on Jennifer's door and introduced the new neighbor, as Jennifer asked them in.

"I'm so sorry to hear about the disappearance of your friend, and I would like to help in any way possible. Is there's anything you need done that I can do?" he offered.

Ellen noted he still held Jennifer's hand and appeared very solicitous of her well-being. She experienced a second of "Hey-I'm-hurting-from-the-loss-too," but quickly chose to ask if he had seen anything at all on the day Bud had disappeared.

Seemingly taken aback at Ellen's interruption, Zack released Jennifer's hand, and after a slight hesitation, as though carefully considering his reply, he said, "Not really. Uh, I told the sheriff everything I know."

Ellen wanted to ask, *Yeah, and what exactly was that?*

Instead she said, "All about how you were speeding too, I suppose." Immediately wishing she had not said it and not wanting to irritate this man further, she forced a chuckle and said, "I really wish you had been a little faster. Perhaps we would have a good description of the black SUV that was in such a hurry."

"Yes," he replied, "it would be good to have some kind of a lead, and a good description might really turn up one."

Jennifer offered tea and all three sat at the table. They began to sort through all the things they *did* know, which admittedly was not much.

The beautiful piece of golden lace with the diamond center was still on the table, and Jennifer handed it to Zack saying, "This may well be a bit of evidence. There's no reason for it to be here. Ellen found it under the edge of the cabinet while cleaning."

Zack took the item, looking it over very carefully, before giving it back to Jennifer, who laid it on the table next to the sugar bowl.

Ellen knew she needed to be going and sensed no further information would be forthcoming from this rather close-mouthed, self-contained neighbor. Further prompting her to leave was the feeling that he was waiting for her to do so. He seemed to be lingering...just sort of passing the time. What else could he be waiting for? Maybe he had something that he wanted only Jennifer to hear. That seemed absurd.

*Good gosh*, thought Ellen, *I'm just too tired to think reasonably.*

Excusing herself, she left. She noted that Zack accepted another glass of tea. Why did she feel he knew more than he was disclosing?

Ellen hurriedly fed Seizer, Miss Muffy and Old Yowler as soon as she reached her house. Realizing she was late with Baby's bottle, she added extra milk and went to see if Baby were at the barn gate.

Her orphaned calf was very special to Ellen. Baby's mother had narrowed airways and could not get enough oxygen to support her needs. After Baby was born, the condition worsened. She died on the fifth day after giving birth, and Baby was torn between leaving her

21

mother's side and coming to Ellen, her substitute provider. Ellen let her remain with her mother for a couple of days and just took her a bottle three times a day. Baby soon learned her mother was gone forever and started following Ellen around just like a puppy.

Ellen knew she needed to be with others of her own kind, so eventually she put Baby with the herd, taking her bottles as usual.

If Ellen were late for a feeding, Baby would find her way back to the barn gate. Occasionally, they happened to meet somewhere along the path. Ellen could hardly see Baby moving through the tall grass; she was so tiny and was always very intent upon following the path. Seeing Baby all alone, hurrying, with her nose close to the ground, lost in the tall grass, maybe even prey to a stray dog or coyote, Ellen was overcome with sympathy and a desire to protect her. She loved this little creature and would give her the best of care.

When Ellen reached the barn gate, Baby was there, nervously pacing back and forth with an occasional protesting bawl. Ellen sank to her knees, offering the warm milk. Baby couldn't drink it fast enough, gulping and blowing bubbles. The half-gallon of milk disappeared quickly. Ellen put her arm around her and rubbed down her coat, all the while telling her she was sorry to be late. Ellen loved her animals. They were almost like children to her.

Knowing Baby would never go back to the herd alone and with darkness upon them, Ellen walked out into the pasture to find the rest of the cows. Baby followed close behind. She always had to linger with the herd until Baby was distracted; else the calf would follow her back to the barn. Ellen found the way back to her house by moonlight and was finally able to enjoy her own food and drink, trying not to gulp as hungrily as Baby had.

Sometime later, after thinking through the events of the day, Ellen called to check on Jennifer and to ask if she had learned anything else from the "mighty fine neighbor."

She was somewhat concerned when Jennifer did not answer the phone. But she decided, as tired as she had been, Jennifer could probably sleep through an F4 tornado. Thinking she needed sleep herself, Ellen gave up and went to bed, sincerely hoping an F4 tornado did not occur.

# Chapter 3

The following morning, Ellen finished her daily routine and decided to check on Jennifer. She also intended to take the piece of jewelry she had found to the sheriff's office. Maybe he would have some information to share.

As Ellen topped the hill just above Bud's driveway, she saw Zack's burgundy truck speeding towards her. Had he just come out of Bud's driveway? She couldn't be sure. As they met, he acknowledged her presence with a slight incline of his head—which she ignored. She told herself, firmly if not convincingly, he had not come from Jennifer's driveway.

Jennifer answered the door. She seemed much more in control of herself and looked rested. She stood staring at Ellen, almost apologetically, as though she wanted to say something, but didn't.

"Got the coffee on? I didn't bother making a pot. I was too busy. So I need my morning fix."

"No, I haven't made any yet." Jennifer blinked and looked away.

"Well, I'll make the coffee while you start your breakfast."

"I've had breakfast already."

"What? Breakfast without coffee?" *That seems unusual,* thought Ellen.

"Uh, oh I wasn't too hungry. Just a bite of toast."

*Exceedingly curious*, thought Ellen. *No coffee with toast?* Oh well, she had just done the same thing herself.

"Okay, then. Skip the coffee. Did the cunning neighbor divulge any more info last night?'

Jennifer seemed somewhat flustered and asked,

"Why do you say 'cunning'?"

"Just a play on words, Jen. His name is Cunningham. He's not much of a ham though. Seems like a smile would crack his face."

"He's really quite a nice man."

Somewhat irritated with Jennifer's defense of Zack, Ellen asked rather sharply, "Did he enlighten you any about Bud's disappearance?"

Jennifer became more agitated than ever. *I need to be more considerate of her,* thought Ellen. *She's been through hell and may even be pregnant.*

"I'm sorry, Jen. Forgive me…I'm just obsessed."

Jennifer smiled and hugged Ellen. Ellen noted, however, that Jennifer had averted her eyes, as she apologetically conveyed she had learned nothing else she could add to what Ellen already knew.

*Nothing more she could add…or would add? Did she learn something she wouldn't tell?*

*I'm getting paranoid,* Ellen told herself. *I need to get a grip.*

"I thought we could take a run into the sheriff's office to see if he has learned anything new. And we can take that diamond thingee for his perusal. Okay? He can't get any fingerprints or DNA off of it though…we've handled it to death."

Jennifer's face lost all color. She hesitated, walked into the kitchen and stared at the table. "I thought the thing was left here on the table, but I don't see it," she said.

Ellen was horrified. She immediately started looking under the table, in the sugar bowl and in the sink basket.

"Where could it have gone? Did you wipe it up and drop it in the trash?" she asked, hurrying to check the wastebasket.

"No, I don't think so. I folded some clothes there

last night. Let me check my drawer." She hurried to the bedroom and returned shortly.

"No, it's not there," she replied, looking guilty and apologetic.

Ellen was devastated. Seemingly the only piece of possible evidence they had found was now gone—had disappeared. How? And Jennifer…why did she look so guilty?

*Good gosh,* Ellen chastised herself. *Of course Jennifer looks guilty. It was left in her care. She feels responsible.* She hugged Jennifer, saying, "Never mind. We'll go see the sheriff anyway."

Only later, driving home, did she connect the fact that Jennifer's face blanched *before* she went into the kitchen and found the piece of jewelry missing. She knew it was gone before she had looked.

Ellen wondered if the cunning mighty fine neighbor had lingered for a reason, other than to offer a helping hand to Jennifer. To pocket a small piece of evidence? Maybe. But why? Had he been involved in Bud's disappearance? Ellen was somewhat distraught. Being suspicious of those around her made her uncomfortable.

When they arrived at the sheriff's office, everyone seemed to be busy with various other problems. Ellen and Jennifer stood for several minutes at the front desk.

Ellen noticed a deputy at the back of the room get up from his desk. Leaving another woman sitting there, he came forward to greet them.

"Good morning," he smiled cordially. Ellen noted the white, even teeth he displayed and the beautiful tan he sported. She thought she recognized him as one of the deputies who had come to Bud's house when the sheriff's team responded to her call.

"Ms. Wade, isn't it?" he asked, as he extended his hand. "I'm Deputy Brady."

"Good morning," she answered, "How are you?

Yes, I am Ellen Wade. And this is Jennifer Phillips."
She motioned to Jennifer. "We would like to speak with
Sheriff Hewitt if it is at all possible."

"Of course," he replied courteously. "He's with
someone right now. If you care to wait, it shouldn't be
long."

"Alright, thank you."

"Just have a seat over there." He indicated a leather
couch near the window. "Would you ladies care for a
cup of coffee while you wait?"

"I would love one," answered Ellen.

So Ellen ended up enjoying her morning "fix" after
all. And Jennifer seemed to enjoy hers as well.

During the twenty or thirty minute wait, Ellen
noticed the deputy looking in her direction often.

Jennifer picked up on it too. She quietly whispered,
"I think he likes you. He's a real good-looking hunk
too, isn't he? Fits his uniform real nice!"

Ellen kind of thought so too, but had other things on
her mind.

The sheriff was finally able to see them. He was
quick to report that he had received some of the
forensic information.

"You'll be happy to hear that the larger pools of
blood were of type O positive. Not your brother's type.
His is AB positive. Only a small sampling of blood on
the door handle, one bloody hand towel in the kitchen
and a few splatters on the floor were AB positive."

Not knowing all the conclusions the sheriff might
draw from those reports, Ellen asked, "What does that
really tell us?"

"Well," drawled the sheriff, "someone—maybe
your brother—caused significantly more damage to
someone else. Course that don't tell us who or how
many others were there or who took who where. All it
tells us is that your brother didn't lose enough blood at

the scene to be alarmed about. 'Course there's always blunt force trauma to contend with, but looks like the other guy got the worst of it. There was a lot of blood loss, and anyone with that amount of loss could not have overpowered anyone all by himself."

Ellen stared at the Sheriff thinking, *Yeah, but we know that there had to be others there because Bud's gone. His vehicles are still at his house, and he's nowhere to be found. Surely he was taken by force, being kept against his will.*

"We don't have too much to go on at this point."

Ellen told the Sheriff about the small gold lace circle with the diamond center that they had discovered and then lost.

"Could be a lady was present during all the commotion," offered the Sheriff.

"Don't forget the mighty fine neighbor had access to that evidence," Ellen exclaimed.

Ellen noticed that Jennifer seemed to shrink and draw into herself at the mention of Zack's possible involvement.

"Of course, we'll consider all possibilities," said the sheriff. "Was your brother about to lose his property and his part of your business?"

Surprised, Ellen queried, "What are you talking about?"

"Records show his wife, one Lila Wade, is suing one Robert B. Wade for divorce, claiming adultery and asking for all property and business interests, bank accounts, etc."

Ellen was alarmed and dumbfounded. "That witch! She'll not do this to him again. She sued for divorce two years ago. And not that he had to, but he gave her all that he had at that time. He didn't even own this property then; nor was he in business of any kind."

The sheriff shrugged his heavy shoulders, pulled at

the corners of his graying mustache and replied, "There is no record of a divorce granted two years ago. *This* petition was filed Wednesday, March 19th. Last month."

"But I know he signed divorce papers about two years ago, and he did tell me that he was divorced some time later. In fact, my ex-husband was her attorney," Ellen exclaimed. "Bud didn't have an attorney. He didn't even show up at the hearing. Lila told him she had filed the papers, and they were divorced. I know she is now saying she never filed the divorce papers and the case was dismissed. I don't think Bud has seen her once since that time, until last month when she showed up claiming to still be his wife. He believed himself to be single. He had found someone else. If the petition is claiming adultery, he didn't know. He thought he was divorced."

Sheriff Hewitt reached into his shirt pocket and retrieved his small pipe. Saying nothing, he stuck it between his teeth, seemingly considering what he had just been told. He further infuriated Ellen with a question about her and not Lila. "Your name is Wade, same as your brother's, but you were married at that time?"

"Yes! We divorced," Ellen exploded. "I took back my maiden name. I didn't want a life time of miserable reminders—being called by his name. This is a crock!"

Enraged, extremely frustrated, scarcely able to control her anger, Ellen wondered what devastation Lila would cause this time.

In an effort to defend Bud, Ellen continued to elaborate upon the circumstances of Bud's divorce. "Lila wanted all Bud had at that time. And he gave it all to her—just to keep the peace and be done with it. He left and joined the service, thinking he was single. Shortly thereafter, our parents were killed in that horrible F4 tornado. Bud and I both inherited a substantial amount from their estate. Lila must have delayed filing the divorce papers, hoping to gain more. She surely had to know of his inheritance. Please say she cannot come back now and rob him again."

Sheriff Hewitt seemed sympathetic and listened carefully to Ellen while Jennifer said nothing and looked as though she wanted to disappear.

Ellen wanted to cry, to beat the wall—or preferably someone who was causing all this chaos. Was Lila behind Bud's disappearance? She would be happy to beat that witch to a pulp. But how would Lila benefit from Bud's disappearance? Wouldn't a divorce work just as well? Had she changed her mind and decided murder was better? Faster? More lucrative, maybe?

Knowing of no other reason to stay, Ellen thanked the sheriff and reluctantly rose to leave.

Sheriff Hewitt also rose and took her hand. "Ms. Wade, I'm confident we'll find your brother, and I am sure all of this will turn out okay. Just rest assured we will find those responsible and make them pay."

He really seemed convinced that everything would indeed turn out alright. Knowing no more than she did, Ellen couldn't say she felt the same way. Did the Sheriff know something he was not telling her? Why would he keep any information from her?

As Ellen and Jennifer exited the building, Deputy Brady opened the door for them and walked beside them down the steps toward the parking lot.

"I'm so sorry for all this hurtful trouble you're having. I know what pain and fear you must be feeling. Please rest assured we're doing all we can to find your brother. And let us know if you think of anything else that might be helpful, or if anything unusual happens."

Ellen felt his concern was genuine and thanked him, promising to do as he asked.

As an afterthought, he asked if she were ready to open her business and start selling all the plants she had been growing.

"Well, yes," she answered, somewhat surprised that he knew anything about her business. "But right now I'm only selling wholesale to other suppliers, not to the general public."

"Oh....well, I have always been interested in the nursery business and would really enjoy seeing your operation sometime. Perhaps when you are not too busy to be bothered."

Taken aback and not knowing how to respond to his request, Ellen said, "Of course, ...of course, but call before you come. I am pretty busy right now, and I transport to several vendors, so I'm not always at home."

Driving away, Jennifer laughed, "I told you he was interested in you. He didn't waste any time, did he?"

"He seems really nice and very good-looking, but too perfect somehow," answered Ellen.

Sometime later when Ellen was out watering her plants and adjusting the air flow through the green houses, she saw Zack's burgundy Ford pass her drive. In approximately ten minutes, it drove past in the opposite direction.

He could have gone no farther than Jennifer's. No one else lived close down that road.

Had he delivered her a message? Was it about Bud? She lingered close to the phone, hoping to hear from Jennifer and find out what Mr. "Cunning" had to say.

After perhaps an hour, Ellen could stand it no longer. She called Jennifer's number and got no answer. Puzzled, she wondered if Jennifer were sleeping through her phone calls or was she not at home? Had Zack picked her up instead of delivering a message?

With a sinking feeling, Ellen went about her regular

duties: repotting, fertilizing and planting other seeds including some of her best sellers—flowers.

Curiously mulling over the questions in her mind, Ellen asked herself why she should think Zack possessed more information about Bud. There was no reason to assume that. It was just a feeling she had that wouldn't go away. He knew something he wasn't telling. Pushing aside those bothersome thoughts, as she usually tried to do, she decided he had most probably picked up Jennifer for a visit—or maybe she was not even at home. She sometimes drove Bud's vehicles. That must be it. It would account for his short time there.

Unable to resist and knowing she was behaving like an intruder, Ellen got into her pick-up and drove the short distance to her brother's house. Both of his vehicles were there. So if Jennifer were not at home, in all probability, Zack had picked her up.

Ellen knocked loudly several times and called out to Jennifer. No one answered.

Maybe someone else had taken Jennifer somewhere before Zack had arrived, but Ellen was pretty sure Zack *had* come by. She was curious about just why. More puzzled than ever, Ellen wondered why Zack was so persistently with Jennifer. Admittedly, she was attractive, but this was a little soon, was it not? And what about Jennifer? She was or should be married to Bud and was most likely carrying his child. Did Jennifer find Zack that attractive? She remembered the soft curl of his hair, the blue of his eyes, the strong, square-shouldered physique and the very confident way he carried himself.

"Not a bad package," she mused, "if one could put up with his disagreeable, closed-mouth attitude." Anyone would think he had something to hide.

Since Ellen was so busy all the time, Jennifer was

pretty much always alone. Jennifer surely needed someone to talk to and be with, but why Zack? She did have other friends. Zack must feel compelled to look after her welfare. Ellen had to admit it would be nice to have someone around to help once in awhile.

"Guess there's nothing wrong with that," she muttered.

Still she was apprehensive and kind of felt left out...kind of pushed aside. It was a distinctly unpleasant feeling.

Ellen shrugged her shoulders, telling herself whatever the reason, she guessed it was Jennifer's business, and she should let well enough alone. But why did they seem so secretive about the whole thing?

*Are they weaving tangled webs or am I just being paranoid?*

# Chapter Four

The next evening when Ellen went to give Baby her bottle, she discovered a section of her fence destroyed, flat on the ground. It was on the border between her property and Zack's.

"Good Glory," she exclaimed, wondering what disaster had taken such a toll.

When she spied her herd among the trees in the shade, she noticed an extra bovine creature among them. Huge and dark red, likely a Beefmaster, the awesome bull was lying there, contentedly chewing his cud.

"I do not need this!" complained Ellen. How could she get him out of her pasture? *All my cows are bred. Based on that, he should not wish to linger, but readily go back to his own herd. So maybe getting him out is do-able,* she thought.

She hurriedly fed Baby and decided repairing the fence was first priority. *Just leave a hole for him to go through that could quickly be closed off once he left,* she reasoned. *Hope he won't need too much persuasion to go through that hole.* She was glad she had fed her cattle a little earlier. It gave her more time before darkness set in to make the needed repairs.

She hurried back to get her truck, loaded it with posts, a post driver, clips, plus extra wire, wire ties and wire stretchers. *And don't forget the cubes,* she cautioned herself.

Returning to the pasture, she straightened out the broken-down fence, removing all the posts from it. Then she drove them back into the proper line, putting in several extras for added strength. Two posts driven closely together might, hopefully, hold the wire taut so she could stretch it properly. Leaving an approximate six-foot opening, she clipped the barbed wires back to the posts, starting with the top wire first to reduce the likelihood of tangling strands as she progressed.

After an hour and a half, she parked her truck at an angle on one side of the opening and took a bucket of cubes from her truck. She started spreading cubes up to and through the opening. Calling her cows, she hoped she could keep them from going through the opening in the fence, while letting the big red dude continue picking up cubes and munching his way through—not realizing what was happening.

The "papa cow" stood and stretched, as one by one, the rest of the herd did the same. He was not only awesome, he was fearsome. Ellen's determination wavered momentarily. *But stretching is good*, she thought. *Supposed to indicate good health. And maybe a relaxed attitude, as well*, she hoped. She would have to be extremely careful here. She did not know how tame he was, and he might just resent her attempt to send him home. Her cows, however, were gentle and very accustomed to Ellen's presence; they came confidently to the sprinkling of cubes.

To scoot them aside and let the big dude through was the trick. Ellen grabbed a long stick. As inconspicuously as possible, so as not to spook the herd, she poked and prodded each cow that got in front of him before he reached the opening. Finally, he was there. Ellen slipped around the truck and was now behind him. He was almost through the opening when he seemed to hesitate and started to turn back.

Ellen grabbed her courage. Yelling as loud as she could, she whacked the big guy across the rump. Startled, he jumped all the way through the opening, and Ellen hurriedly picked up the ends of the wires she had left lying on the ground, fastening them across the opening. She tied the top, middle and bottom, then started stretching all six strands as tightly as possible, hopefully securing them permanently.

"Big Daddy" ate all the cubes on his side of the fence and was sniffing for more. Gathering up her tools, Ellen was gratified he had not resisted. It had actually been easier than she had expected. He watched as she drove away, and Ellen heard him bellow his resentment, much like a bull elephant, as she pulled her truck back inside her yard.

"Stay on your side of the fence, big fellow. You didn't have an invitation, and all the ladies on this side won't have need of male companionship for a good while yet," she muttered.

Ellen decided to call Zack and let him know his cattle sire had breached their mutual fence. She called information for his new number. There was not one listed so she decided to drive to his house and tell him in person.

As she entered his driveway, she saw Zack and a young woman exit his truck. Zack's truck was blocking Ellen's view of the woman for the most part, but Ellen thought the flash of blond, honey-colored hair matched Jennifer's to a T. The woman entered Zack's open garage door and disappeared before Ellen got close enough to be certain. Zack turned and came toward Ellen's vehicle as she opened her door and stepped out.

He casually greeted her. "Evening, Ms. Wade."

"How are you?" she asked. He considered it a return greeting, she supposed, as he did not reply.

"I just wanted to let you know that your big...uh..." She didn't want to say "bull" because some people, especially women, thought it inappropriate for a woman to say the word. *Why? How different was it from saying "rooster"? And they say "cock," (like in the cock crows) don't they? That's more vulgar sounding than bull, isn't it?* wondered Ellen.

"Um, your Beefmaster—I suppose Beefmaster—sire took out part of our common fence line and was in with my herd," she finished.

"Oh, Old Rogue! Does pretty much what he wants to. I'm sorry. I'll get him out first thing tomorrow," he apologized. A soft dark curl seemed out of place on his forehead as though fingers had played in his hair. "Old Rogue" might fit Mr. Cunning, as well.

"No need," she informed him. "I got him back through and mended the fence. All my cows are registered Limousins, and I don't really want any crosses. All my cows are bred though so no harm done. I did mend the fence, but in all likelihood he will do it again."

"And you did all this by yourself?" he asked, as though he didn't believe her.

She stared at him for a second, feeling a sliver of resentment.

Abruptly she said, "I did indeed, Mr. Cunning, or...uh...Mr. Cunningham." She couldn't call him Zack though Jennifer did. They were not on familiar enough terms for that, though calling him Mr. Cunningham sounded a trifle stilted. Mr. "Cunning" really seemed to fit better. "We may need a better fence between us before calving time. Just thought I should let you know. Good fences make good neighbors and all that," she continued.

He was staring at her now. An almost smile on his lips and maybe a flicker of something new in his eyes. *What was it?* she wondered. *Respect, disbelief or just plain curiosity? Maybe ridicule.*

"We have plenty of time so we can discuss it more later if you like."

He was still staring and did not reply until she said, "Have a good evening," and turned to go.

She heard him answer, "Yes, yes of course, whenever you're ready," as she hurried to her truck.

She drove by to see if Jennifer were at home. Jennifer was not. Ellen felt an uncomfortable stirring in the pit of her stomach.

The following morning the phone rang as Ellen was just starting out to water her plants. It was Deputy Brady.

"I have the day off and wondered if it might be a good time to see your operation?"

"Uh...well... okay...yes, I guess so," stuttered Ellen. This was sooner than she had expected. She wasn't even sure he had been serious when he mentioned coming by.

"I was just starting to water a few plants, but I'll wait a bit, and I'll even put on the coffee pot."

"That would be great." His reply was enthusiastic.

He showed up in blue jeans and a white shirt and looked just as attractive as he had in uniform. Jennifer was right. He was a good-lookin' hunk. She was never fond of crew cuts, but this one looked good on him.

He had brought apple fritters.

"How did you know I love apple fritters?"

"I have inside information." He laughed. His eyes crinkled. "No, not really," he hastily corrected himself, "I just love them too."

Later, over coffee and the apple fritters, they discussed the disappearance of Bud. He had nothing else to add, but closely questioned Ellen about any details, no matter how small, that might shed some light on why Bud would be a target or who might want something from him. The only person Ellen could think of was Lila, but that seemed far-fetched so she did not mention her. His questioning seemed intense to her, and she wondered if that were his primary motive for the visit, not any interest in gardening. Or was he just trying to convince her that the sheriff's department looked under every stone?

Finally, they toured the premises, and Ellen showed him her setup, how the irrigation, heating and ventilation systems worked. He listened closely and seemed to be very interested. She showed him her posted schedules: when to plant certain seeds and what temperature should be maintained for each, exactly what soil components were used and how much fertilizer, when it should be applied, how much sunlight and when to increase or decrease it, when to trim and when to re-pot or re-plant.

"It really is quite time-consuming, isn't it?" He seemed impressed.

"Yes, it is and lots more work than one would imagine and requires quite a bit of knowledge, as well as luck with the weather, competition, marketing strategies, etc.," she concluded. He agreed.

Ellen realized she had enjoyed his visit more than expected and felt gratified that he thought she was doing a good job. Lots of people thought farming a snap and that only those who could do nothing else chose to farm. They should all try it. Only those who really loved it would ever stick with it. The work was too hard and the income too iffy.

It was much easier to take a job where the boss says, "Here's what has to be done and here is how to do it. And here is how much you will be paid each week."

As he was leaving, he asked if she were going to the charity dance being held at the Country Club the following Friday evening.

"No. I had not heard they were having one," she replied.

"I would be honored—more like tickled pink—if you would accompany me. It's a dinner and dance and starts at 7 p.m.," he said with a grin.

Her first impulse was to say no, but it occurred to her that she might enjoy an evening out. Jennifer was obviously busy with who knows what, and what would it hurt anyway? Maybe she could use him as a conduit for information from the sheriff's office about Bud.

"I've not danced in centuries," she said. "But if you care to take on the challenge, I will." She laughed.

"Great," he said. "I'll pick you up here at 6:30 Friday evening."

"Okay. By the way, what do I call you? Mr. Deputy, Deputy Brady or do you have a front name?"

"Ron," he grinned, and his eyes crinkled at the corners.

"I think I may like this guy," Ellen told herself.

The rest of the week was the usual workload, but Ellen managed to ferret out an evening dress and bought new shoes and a bottle of *Design,* her favorite perfume. She even made an appointment at Maggie's Hair Salon for a "new do."

*Golly,* she thought, *I've not acted like a woman for so-oo long. All I wear anymore are blue jeans and sweatshirts.*

She called the sheriff's office on two occasions to inquire about any new information concerning Bud. She actually was able to speak directly with Sheriff Hewitt himself on both occasions.

"No, we really don't have much else I can tell you," he drawled.

Did the word *can* have significance? Did he mean, *I know more, but that's all I can tell you?*

Ellen was exasperated. He seemed so unconcerned.

On the second call, he did, however, say they might have a lead.

"Now, little lady," he cheerfully stated, "you need to just let us do our job, and we will let you know if we come up with something. We do have a lead and it looks promising. I think your brother is okay."

Ellen's heart skipped a beat. *Oh, glory* she thought. "What kind of a lead?" she asked. "Has he contacted you? Is he hurt?"

"Now, little lady, I can't divulge our information yet, but as soon as possible, I'll let you know."

Disheartened, Ellen hung up the phone. Was Sheriff Hewitt giving her a bunch of crap just to keep her from bothering him? Not knowing was so hard to handle.

One out-of-the-ordinary occurrence did happen late on Thursday morning. The phone rang and Ellen was flabbergasted when she heard Lila's voice purring, "Good morning, Ell. Got a minute?"

Ellen wanted to say absolutely not, but curiosity had got the better of her and she said, "Just barely." She waited to hear what Lila wanted.

"Just thought since you're giving tours, you might show me through your greenhouses and all." Ron must have told her of his visit. That further irritated Ellen. She didn't like being the topic of a conversation between them.

"Now why would I do that, Lila? You know you're not welcome here."

"You may as well get used to me being around, you know. Since I'm still Bud's wife and he is your partner, that gives me some inalienable rights I intend to exercise."

"You are not Bud's wife until the courts say you are, and you had better not show up here or I will exercise *my* inalienable rights, which you may find very unpleasant," countered Ellen, slamming down the phone.

Uneasiness worked its way into her thinking that hung on throughout the day. What if, by hook or crook, that witch actually became her partner? Had Lila sent

Ron to gather information about Ellen's business?

It had been a few days since Ellen had noticed Zack's truck going to Jennifer's, and for some reason she felt relieved. But early one morning as she was going into Malden to do some shopping, Ellen saw Zack drive out from the road a mile south of hers and turn onto the one leading to his house. As they met and passed, Ellen could see a woman beside him. She knew it was Jennifer.

*So*, she thought, *he is still picking her up but going to her house around the section line—in the back way. Why? So I wouldn't know! But why? They shouldn't want to hide an innocent relationship from me.*

Her heart sank. *Now really, Ellen*, she chided herself. *Could this be an innocent relationship?* They were together constantly, it seemed. *What a horrible thing for Bud. How could Jennifer do such a thing to him, especially since she might be carrying his child.* Ellen tried not to think of Jennifer and Zack, but it was difficult. Seemed like rogue behavior to her. Wasn't Zack invading someone else's pasture?

Ellen tried hard to finish all her work and do all her chores early on Friday afternoon so she could properly ready herself for her first dinner engagement in quite some time. She kept her mid-afternoon salon appointment and was surprised at her appearance upon seeing herself with an elegant upsweep. The large lustrous curls and twists made her look at least two inches taller. She laughed out loud as she was getting her nails manicured. *What would Baby think?* Asking such a question told her how much she had cut herself off from outside activities in the last few years.

She hurried home to bathe and dress. She had chosen a sleeveless, full length white gown with small gathers at each shoulder and a plunging neckline, but not too plunging. The full circle skirt hung beautifully and swung gracefully above a pair of orange high heel pumps on sleek ankles that made her look even taller. Ellen had chosen orange for her accessories because of her tan. Orange lipstick seemed to compliment her tan best. The white dress seemed to darken the tan. She fastened an orange sash around her small waist. It flowed almost to her knees and complemented her orange shoes.

She became somewhat concerned as she realized she did not have an appropriate handbag. What to do? She remembered Jennifer's small sequined, white clutch. That would do fine.

Though she had been avoiding Jennifer as much as possible of late, Ellen called to see if she could borrow the clutch.

"Of course. I'd be delighted to lend it to you," Jennifer said, eager to please.

Ellen hurried over to pick it up, noting she was about to run out of time.

Jennifer gasped as Ellen entered the room, "Oh, God, you look absolutely gorgeous," she exclaimed. "Where are you going?"

"To the Country Club Charity Dinner-Dance with Ron Brady," replied Ellen, pleased by Jennifer's compliment. "And I don't have a minute to spare."

Thanking Jennifer and promising to return the bag soon, Ellen flew out the door straight into the arms of a stunned "mighty fine neighbor" who drove a burgundy truck.

Zack was caught off-guard, as was Ellen, and struggled to keep his balance and then struggled to catch her as she attempted to stop and stumbled backward.

His arms closed around her. He pulled her firmly to him as he asked with concern, "Are you okay?"

"Yes…I'm okay," she answered.

Obviously astonished, he loosened his grip and stared, looking at her hair, the length of her dress, the glow of her skin, while the subtle scent of her perfume invaded the air space around him. His eyes lingered on her mouth.

Though barely audible, Ellen heard the "Wow!" he uttered.

Wiggling out of his grip, she repeated, "I'm fine. I'm fine. Sorry…I didn't…uh, expect you. Forgive me. I have to run."

She hurried quickly to her Honda. As she opened her car door, she distinctly heard him ask Jennifer, "What was that?"

Laughing, Jennifer replied, "That's Ellen in a hurry to keep a dinner date with Ron Brady."

Ellen never looked back as she sped away, but somehow she knew he was still watching her as she left.

She had a few moments to compose herself before Ron arrived. He was dressed in a very nice, dark suit and tie with highly polished boots, she noticed.

*Law enforcement officers and military personnel always have perfectly shined footwear,* she thought.

"You are absolutely beautiful," he told her, and his eyes unabashedly took her in from head to toe.

"Thanks, you look pretty good yourself," she said lightly.

Dinner was lovely, and the dancing was very enjoyable with only a minor misstep or two. The only unpleasantness during the evening was caused by Bud's ex, Lila.

She approached their table, wearing a glamorous, if somewhat revealing evening gown. "Ron, my sweet, aren't you going to ask me to dance?" she asked, putting her hand on the back of his neck and pressing up against his chair.

Ron's tan darkened somewhat. Seemingly flustered, he said, "Well, I...uh...didn't see you, but I pretty much had my arms full already...and pleasantly so."

Lila smiled, but not with her eyes, and said that she would forgive him if he rectified that oversight—or slight—immediately.

Ron clearly did not want to leave Ellen alone at the table, but at that moment an elderly gentleman approached and asked to squire Ellen around the floor. She had noticed him watching her from time to time throughout dinner. She accepted his offer, mostly to alleviate the tension, and tried not to notice as Lila draped herself all over Ron on the dance floor.

Overall, the evening was very pleasant, but Ellen was glad when it was over.

"Thank you for a very fun evening. I enjoyed it very much, and I am totally exhausted," Ellen told Ron as he walked her to her door.

"I am so glad you said yes when I asked. I was afraid you wouldn't. And it was your company that made the evening so enjoyable," Ron answered as he gathered her close in his arms and gave her a soft lingering kiss. But it was Zack's arms she felt around her, and she wondered what his kisses would be like.

Later when she was trying to fall asleep, Ellen wondered why Zack had shown up at Jennifer's door in the evening. It wasn't the first time he had picked her up late in the day though. Why did they not want Ellen to know? Was she staying all night at his house? Ellen knew she was.

And then there was Ron and Lila. Just what was their relationship? Lila seemed to think she had an intimate bond with him. Did she? Ellen sighed heavily as the phrase, *Oh what tangled webs we weave...,* once again entered her mind, niggling its way into her dreams.

# Chapter Five

Absorbed in thoughts of cause and effect concerning Bud's disappearance, Ellen intensely scrutinized every detail of all the facts she had available. She concluded there were only two possibilities: either Lila was behind this maddening nightmare or it was a completely random act. Ellen could not fathom anyone else wishing her brother harm. Based on that premise, she considered what she could do. If it were a random act, there was really nothing she could pursue. There was nowhere to start, no one to question or to watch. But Ellen had to do something. Even if she were digging in the wrong direction, she might come up with a clue of some kind. She was already suspicious of Lila, and she *could* do some checking on her. It was at least a place to start.

More than one person had to have been involved; therefore, Lila must have had some help. So who were her associates? Ron had been. Was he still? Maybe Ellen should have let Lila stick around, perhaps even taunting her until she gave up a broad hint as to what had happened to Bud.

Was Ron still seeing Lila, and did he insinuate himself into Ellen's life in order to find out what she knew about her brother's whereabouts? If so, that meant they didn't know where he was either. It also meant they were not holding him hostage somewhere; they had not murdered him and disposed of his body. That, on the surface, seemed good news. But where was he? Someone had to know.

Ron was a deputy. He theoretically knew everything the sheriff did and therefore everything Ellen knew and probably more. So what did she know that he didn't know? Something he really needed to know? Ellen couldn't imagine what that might be. Would Sheriff Hewitt deliberately withhold information from a deputy? That would be difficult. He would have to withhold it from all deputies, based on their fraternization, wouldn't he? And if the sheriff suspected Lila, and he knew that she and Ron had been close, what then? Would he suspect Ron of being involved in Bud's disappearance? That seemed extremely remote, but Ellen would probe for clues as opportunities presented themselves. She decided to spend more time with Ron and Lila if possible.

The ringing of the phone next to her elbow caused Ellen to start. She spilled coffee in her lap as she reached to answer it.

It was Jennifer. "Sorry to bother you, Ell, but could I borrow one of your vehicles today? I have a doctor's appointment, and neither one of Bud's will start."

Ellen wondered why Zack had not been Johnny-on-the-spot when Jennifer needed a car. He must have had an unusually important, prior commitment.

"Of course," she answered. "What's wrong with Bud's car? Probably a dead battery. It's been setting there a while and not driven."

"That's probably it."

"I will bring battery cables and put it on charge for you. That way you'll have it if you need it later. And I was going into Malden anyway, so I'll be happy to take you to your appointment."

Jennifer hesitated, but finally agreed that would work.

*She must have wanted to run other errands*, thought Ellen as she hung up. *Well, shoot, she should have said so.*

Ellen hurriedly slipped into a clean pair of jeans, then picked up her battery cables and an extension cord, thinking, *Now we'll know for certain if Jen's pregnant, and perhaps she'll stay at home and knit or something. At least, maybe she'll remember whose child it is she's carrying and not be so happy to be with Zack. Bud deserved better than that!*

When Ellen dropped Jennifer off at her doctor's office, she said, "Think I'll drop by and interrogate the sheriff before doing my grocery shopping and stuff. Might as well let them know we're not going away and that we are expecting some answers from them."

"Right on!" Jennifer chuckled.

"We don't really have a suspect, but we're looking at a couple of people of interest," Sheriff Hewitt told Ellen. "Now I can't divulge any information and thereby jeopardize the integrity of the case. We'll let you know, little lady."

Thanking him and thinking, *same old stuff*, Ellen started to leave. Feeling a supporting hand on her elbow, she turned to see Ron Brady open the door. He walked with her to her car.

"Would you like to have lunch with me? The Malden Diner is having their steak special today and it's usually great."

*Here's an opportunity to find out how close he and Lila are*, thought Ellen, *but I can't take the time.*

Jennifer would be waiting so she asked for a rain check saying, "I'd love to, but I have to pick up Jennifer at the doctor's office in an hour, so maybe another time."

"Oh, is Jennifer sick?"

*Why did I have to say that?* "Not really. Just a checkup."

He gave her a long look and then very quietly asked, "Is she in a family way, perhaps?"

Ellen was surprised at the question. It was inappropriate. "Oh, no. I don't think so," she said. "She's just stressed out about Bud and everything, I guess."

Ron studied her for a second, stroking his chin, then asked, "Could I call you in a day or so? Maybe we can get together for dinner and a movie or the bingo hall or maybe even miniature golf. There's not really much to do here, but we could watch the sun set." He laughed and his eyes crinkled.

"Certainly. Call me anytime." She smiled. "Thanks for asking."

Jennifer was waiting for her when Ellen returned to the doctor's office. She seemed somewhat tense, but pretty much in control. She offered no information about anything she had learned from the doctor. Ellen wanted very much to know if Bud were going to be a father. She felt she was entitled to know.

Trying to prompt a comment from Jennifer, she asked, "Did the doctor find you to be in good health?"

"Oh yeah, healthy as a horse. Just stressed out a bit and overly anxious."

*She knows what I am really dying to find out. Why doesn't she tell me?* Jennifer wondered.

Feeling some resentment, Ellen finally forced the issue, "Well, are you for sure pregnant or not?"

Jennifer fidgeted a bit and then said, "Yes. Yes, I am, but please, Ell, don't tell anyone. I'm kind of embarrassed, you know, not being married and all."

"Well gosh, Jen, everyone knew you and Bud were together. Nowadays it's a common thing. And besides, everyone will know soon enough anyway."

"I know. I know, but maybe Bud will be back soon, and we will be married before it's told, and I won't be alone then. Please, Ell, just do this for us."

Ellen was surprised that Jennifer was so squeamish

about letting others know. Didn't seem like Jen. *Oh well, pregnant women do unexpected things,* she guessed.

"Well of course, you goose. I'll keep my mouth shut. The announcement is rightfully yours to make. I know that, Jen." She prayed it would be soon and that Bud would be there to announce it with Jennifer.

Jennifer seemed to relax and to lighten up a bit. With a big, rather proud smile, she said, "I'm anxious to know if it's a boy or a girl, but I'll wait until Bud can go with me and we can find out together."

Ellen noted how positive Jennifer was about Bud's return. *That's a good thing,* she thought. *Good for Jen and good for the baby.* She just wished she felt as positive as Jen.

Ellen let Jennifer out at her doorstep, saying, "Let me know if you need Bud's car before tomorrow morning. You can use mine." *Though I expect you have burgundy colored taxi service,* she thought. "The battery's on a slow charge, so I'll be back early tomorrow to take off the cables and re-hook his Camaro."

Seemingly moved and contrite, Jennifer began, "Thanks a lot, Ell. I wish I ..." she stopped suddenly, and tears filled her eyes.

"What? What do you wish, Jen?"

Jennifer hesitated a moment longer before finishing her sentence. "I wish things were back to normal."

Ellen knew that was not exactly what she had intended to say, but replied, "I wish that too, Jen. Maybe things will get better. And soon."

Approaching her house, Ellen thought she heard a car behind her. Looking into her rear-view mirror, she saw a burgundy truck pass her driveway and make its way toward Jennifer's."

"Why doesn't he leave her alone, for heaven's

sake?" she angrily growled. "He acts like a mother hen protecting her chicks!" Soon the word "protect" took root and she began to wonder. *Does he think she needs protecting?*

That was something new to consider. *If Jen needed protecting, her baby would too. Could that be why she didn't want everyone out there to know she was pregnant?*

Ellen parked her car beside a flashy, late model Cadillac in her driveway. She had no idea who it could be until she noticed the license plate number: IB26E4U.

She groaned. "Crap, I be 2 sexy 4 U! That has got to be Lila. Well, I guess I'll get my chance to listen while she prattles. How can I endure another minute around that self-centered, arrogant, amoral witch? But I need to coax her into spilling the beans about Bud's disappearance. Maybe she'll tell me something I need to know."

Ellen felt anger rise within her as she saw Lila inside one of her greenhouses, poking around with a fistful of carnations in her hand. Knowing if she did not show her anger, she would create suspicion, Ellen asked rather sharply, "What right do you think you have to invade my greenhouses?"

She knew exactly what Lila would say and she did.

"I think they are half-mine so this is my right."

Ellen had threatened to do her harm if she came onto her property and wanted sorely to do just that. But she needed to hear her out, to find out all she could about why Lila had come back claiming to still be Bud's wife, and what her full intentions were.

Ellen throttled her emotions and grimly replied, "I don't believe you'll ever be my partner. But I would like to hear any excuse you may have to offer about your failure to file those divorce papers two years ago, and why we have not heard from you since. Come on in; we'll talk."

Once inside, Ellen offered soft drinks, tea or coffee.

As Ellen got glasses, Lila asked, "Got anything to put in this Coke?"

"Yes I do…ice. Help yourself." She motioned to the side-by-side and poured herself a glass of tea. Ellen knew Lila had meant an alcoholic beverage. And she did have rum, but did not offer it.

Lila seated herself on the couch and immediately asked if Ellen had any news of Bud or what had happened to him. Ellen wouldn't have told her even if he had been in the next room. She did, however, admit there was not much for the sheriff to go on, but did not comment on the sheriff's statement about a couple of "persons of interest." She wondered if Ron had already passed that information on to Lila.

Lila, usually pretty chatty, seemed to be on a mission to gather information rather than to give it. Ellen thought maybe she should have offered the rum after all.

"You know, I think I do have some rum if you'd like some in your Coke," she offered.

Lila would. She said, "Yes, that would be grand."

After a few minutes, Lila asked about Jennifer. "I heard they were going to get married. They have been together for a long time, haven't they?"

"I'm not sure how long," Ellen answered and left it at that.

"Maybe she's expecting and that's why they wanted to get married."

This was the second person, who in one day, had shown interest in Jennifer's condition. Had Lila asked because Ron had failed to get a satisfactory answer? Were they in collusion or was Ron sleuthing for the sheriff? Why did they care?

Ellen was in no way going to confirm that. She casually said, "No, I don't think so. They're just crazy about each other." She hoped that hurt Lila a little. "Why didn't you file those divorce papers? You told Bud he was divorced. Why lie?" Ellen continued.

"Well, the papers were signed, and I wasn't in a real big hurry. Then I heard about your parents and the tornado. I didn't want to hurt him any more than he was hurt."

"That's a bunch of crap!" Ellen couldn't help herself. "You told him you had the divorce, that he was single already. He thought that was true. There would have been no more hurt involved. You thought he would inherit half of mom and dad's estate, and you might get your hands on that too, didn't you?"

Lila grinned, "What evil, suspicious thoughts you have Ell. By the way, I had dinner with your ex last week. He's kind'a fallen on hard times lately."

Ellen didn't comment. Her insides lurched. She wanted to slap this witch. Lila had a fling with Harry, Ellen's ex-husband, after Lila had supposedly divorced Bud. Ellen had a hard time with that bit of news. But Lila hadn't been Harry's first self-indulgent episode, not by a long shot. She had, however, been the last straw. That's when Ellen had changed her name from Pierce back to Wade.

*Typical Lila*, thought Ellen. *She loves to boast of a conquest and loves to inflict pain if possible. Doesn't really matter anymore, except she still enjoys alluding to it repeatedly.*

"He asked about you," Lila said with a grin.

Ellen ignored the comment and said, "Seems you and Ron Brady are an item at present, since you snatched him away from me the other night."

Lila laughed, delighted. "Not really, though we did have a thing going. My current heartthrob is a really super cool stud, Carlo Rodriguez. He owns that big horse ranch south of Amber City, the Champion

Stables. Really a neat place. And he puts all other hombres to shame."

"Guess he bought you that snazzy bronze car out front, huh?" queried Ellen.

"Yeah, that and lots more. Expensive jewelry even. He really likes me. It's like having a printing press and the plates to the one hundred dollar bill." Lila laughed. Then she sobered. "For right now at least, some secret agent man called Sid is trying to nail him on bogus charges and send him back to Mexico." Then she laughed again. "They'll never get my Carlo. He's always ahead of the game."

"If you have all you need and more, why are you trying to take what Bud has? Besides, you would hate to live on a farm or do any of the work."

Lila smiled sweetly, "As I said, Carlo is always ahead of the game, but just in case he should lose the game, I need a nest to fall into, you know."

So she was admitting she wanted more from Bud. More was never enough, not for people like Lila.

"By the way, who is that hunk that moved in next to you?' Lila asked.

Ellen was outraged. Zack was another male for Lila to ensnare with her wicked, alluring ways.

"I don't remember his name. I've seen him a couple of times, and he seems like a sourpuss, not at all the party animal you prefer," she answered.

"He's real easy to look at. Some men just need the right woman to loosen them up and show them how to play." Lila grinned and waggled her butt.

Ellen had had enough. "Lila, if you don't mind—or even if you do—I have work to do, so if you have inflicted enough, I'll see you to your car."

"Well! What do you mean, inflicted?"

"You know very well what I mean, Lila, and you are still not welcome here. Stay away or I will get a court order to restrain you."

Indignant, Lila tossed her head, and sneered. "It'll do you no good to get an injunction," she said. "I will just ignore it and come anyway."

Ellen knew that was true, but if there happened to be a confrontation, it would be of record that Lila was, by law, not to be on the premises.

"Anyway, my Carlo is more forceful than any law. He can handle a whole SWAT team with his weapons," boasted Lila.

Ellen wondered exactly what weapons Carlo really had, but she would still seek the injunction. And maybe let the sheriff know about Carlo's weapon stash.

After doing the work Ellen had referred to, she was glad to retire. Trying to put all the thoughts and questions of the day out of her mind and get to sleep, Ellen reluctantly found herself remembering the past and the hurt her ex had left her to endure. She found herself wondering how "hard were the times" he had fallen on. How bad was his situation?

Her mind wouldn't rest. Her thoughts kept going back to their time together. She had thought they were happy, at least in the beginning. But she had eventually seen him as he was. She remembered when they were in college together in psych class. Some of the students were trying to psychoanalyze each other, which was against all rules and regulations. Just for fun though, they wanted to determine their own personalities. Harry was told by several others that he had no personality of his own, that he was bits and pieces of all types. She thought at the time that he was just not revealing his true thoughts and ideas for them to toy with. But after years of wearily trying to understand him, she became aware that they were right. It was true. He really had no personality all his own, because he had no real convictions of his own—at least, none strong enough to keep him from overriding them to please his then current companions. He was waiting and watching others to see how he should react. She could now see how others thought him a paragon of virtue, always in control. Everyone liked him; he thought exactly as they did. The right platitude was always regurgitated. He never got loud or said the wrong thing. Why should he? He had no feelings about it one way or the other, except to say—or do—what would make him look the true model of perfection at any given time. For a time, she had believed he was.

However, she recalled an incident where an employee's wife confronted him about some complaint her husband had about his salary. Harry was unable to get her to shut up, and everyone at the party was gathering to listen.

Harry, for once, lost his cool and said to her husband, "If you can't control your wife, maybe you can't control your responsibilities."

Ellen was flabbergasted. Harry had always touted women's rights. How was it then that he thought men should control their wives?

On many occasions, he had told her, "The way to take control over any person is to keep them off balance."

She eventually learned that she was one of those persons he contrived to keep off balance. It was comically easy for him. He knew which buttons to push, and she was too trusting to think him anything but honest and forthright. She thought they were together, as one, working to make a life for each other. She never suspected manipulation, domination or competition. She had believed he was putting forth his own true thoughts, and when they differed from hers, she thought she was the one out of sync.

In the end, he told her that it was a man's job to keep his wife subservient, that she should honor his superiority. He would not be found remiss in his duty. He would make her reverence his elevated status. She fervently prayed for him then. She prayed that God would give him what he was in the greatest need of. She thought that greatest need would be a substantial kick in the butt...generously sprinkled with some very strong and real emotions. Maybe then he could know the depths of despair into which she had plunged.

But that was some time ago, and she had come to terms with that part of her life. In fact, she now had very few feelings about it or him, probably as unfeeling about it now as he had been then. But it had left her skeptical of men in general and marriage in particular. She knew she would never marry again. It was too risky and certainly not worth the effort to try to please a man.

# Chapter 6

It was Monday morning again, a beautiful sunny morning with the birds expressing their joy at being alive. Old Seizer was chasing a rabbit through the pecan orchard, and Miss Muffy and old Yowler were patiently waiting at the patio door for their breakfast.

Ellen's thoughts were, however, in turmoil. Too much time had passed, and they still knew almost nothing about Bud's disappearance or who had assaulted him. Something had to be done. Surely, someone could help her do something besides sit and wait.

Lila was a problem. Could she actually take all that Bud had now? Would the court grant the divorce without Bud's appearance? Justifiably, that would not be the case. He is missing, not just acquiescing. Someone had to defend him in his absence. She had to get an attorney. She needed some answers, like now. She shuddered to think of Lila as a partner.

Then there was Zack and Jennifer. If they had developed a relationship –and it appeared they had— what about Bud's baby and Bud when they found him? Her heart ached.

What about Ron? Was he the nice guy he seemed to be or was he still attached to Lila and helping her whenever she asked him to? Hopefully not, as Lila herself had said that her fling with him was over and she had a new flame: one Carlo Rodriguez. But Lila had many flings. Who could tell when one was over?

Ellen forced herself to concentrate on the tasks at hand. *Take care of what you can and pray for the best,* she told herself.

After feeding her cats and Old Seizer, Ellen warmed

a bottle for Baby. As soon as she checked her cows, she had to deliver vegetable plants and flowers to several different vendors.

Oklahoma's average last spring frost date was the 20th of April, and growers typically planted as early as they felt it was safe. Ellen usually sold as many of the various plants as possible and planted any leftover in her garden for her own use. If she had more produce than she could use—and she normally did—she would sell the extra.

*Like the Blue Belle Ice Cream people,* she thought, *eat all we can and sell the rest.* Ellen liked the idea.

This morning she would deliver the last of her tomato plants with the exception of four six-packs. That would be enough for her, Bud and Jennifer. Ellen would make sure they all had plenty of tomatoes in the freezer to make lots of vegetable soup during the winter. Bud especially loved it with hot cornbread and garlic butter.

As Ellen approached the herd, she saw that Old Rogue had once again breached the fence and was happily grazing with her contented cows.

"Oh Lord! I don't need another problem, especially this morning." she wailed. She tried to control her emotions, which was becoming more difficult for her. She needed to concentrate on the one-step-at-a-time approach to each day. The next step right then was to distribute her plants.

So Ellen loaded all the flats that she had to deliver, then drove to Zack's house to see if he had any advice to offer about building a fence that would keep his "Old Rogue" out of her pasture.

As she got out of her truck and approached his house, Zack stepped out on the front porch in his stocking feet. He sipped from a cup of steaming coffee in his hand.

*I should ask for a cup of coffee and follow him in just to see how many plates are set on the table,* she mused.

Zack said he had a number of important things to take care of and would be unable to repair the fence for several days. He asked if he could pay pasture rent until then. Ellen was disgusted. What was he doing with all his time anyway? He shouldn't be in the cattle business if he couldn't take care of his animals.

"I would rather it be done now, since Old Rogue will go back and forth, and soon my cows will follow him or all of yours will come over to my pasture. That compromises the integrity of the grass, and I don't have any to spare. Plus, our herds will become mixed and may be hard to separate. If you are willing to pay one half of the expense, I'll hire someone to help me and we'll do it now," Ellen explained.

"I'm sorry I can't help now, but of course I will be happy to pay my share," Zack replied, somewhat chagrined.

Ellen felt an immediate response to his humiliation. She fought the urge to apologize and smooth the curl that stood out from the rest.

They discussed the necessary repairs and agreed to totally replace the section Old Rogue kept going through. "Several posts there should be concreted in, and a gate would be nice to put him back through, in case he finds another vulnerable section," Ellen suggested.

What was that glint in his eyes? Amusement? No... more like...I-know-you-better-than-you-think...kind of a look. What was it about that curl on his forehead? Why couldn't she quit wanting to smooth it back into place? *Maybe I should just whack it off,* she thought.

"That's fine," Zack agreed to her gate proposal.

*Fine for you.* Ellen thought as she wondered who

she would find to help her do all that work.

After dropping off the last of her flats to the vendors, Ellen took time to stop by the sheriff's office. Inquiring about any news concerning Bud, she told the sheriff about Lila's insistence that she had a right to interfere in her business. She also mentioned Lila's remark about Carlo's gun power.

Thoughtfully, Sheriff Hewitt's eyes narrowed. The lines around his mouth tightened as he spoke. "It's probably a good idea for you to get an attorney. James Caldwell on the next block is an exceptionally good one. And I wouldn't do anything to antagonize that Rodriguez bunch. They have a reputation of trying to enforce their own law."

"But you don't let them get away with that, do you?" Ellen asked.

"We do everything we can within the law, little lady," he answered. "But it hardly does the victim any good if we enforce it after the crime." His face took on a rather grim expression. He puffed air through the small pipe stem he held clenched in his teeth.

"Got the point," Ellen replied.

Deputy Brady had been shuffling papers several feet away, and Ellen felt sure he had heard all of her conversation with the sheriff. As she rose and walked to the door, he was there with a smile on his face, offering again to take her to lunch.

"I'm sorry. I would like that very much, but I have to repair a fence. My neighbor's papa cow keeps breaking into my pasture. Do you happen to know anyone who might be in the fencing business that could help me do those repairs?"

"I'm not in the business, but I'm off for the next couple of days and I would be delighted to help," he offered.

"No. Really, this will be a considerable undertaking.

You don't want to give up that much of your time off," she countered.

"Yes, I do!" he laughed. "And I'll be there early. What time?"

Admitting it saved her a lot of time and effort looking for someone else and that it would give her a chance to find out more about his relationship with Lila, she finally consented.

"Eight O'clock. And I'll serve lunch. That is, unless you change your mind and leave before then," she laughed. "How does cold chicken and potato salad strike you?"

"Great," he said.

He walked her to her truck and opened the door for her. She thanked him again and added, "You really are a very nice guy, Ron. I appreciate this a bunch."

He patted her hand and grinned, "My pleasure." He said and sounded as if he meant it.

After picking up all the items on her fence repair list at the lumber yard, Ellen dropped by the office of James Caldwell, Attorney-at-law. He was booked up for several days so Ellen took the first available appointment.

*He must be good if he's that busy,* she assumed. His secretary promised she would call her sooner if they had a cancellation.

Ellen stopped at Love's Country Store for gas on her way home and impulsively bought a candy bar. It was not something she ordinarily did, but she felt the need to treat herself. When she reached her farm, Ellen unloaded all her supplies at the site of the needed fence repairs. She was somewhat tired and promised herself a short nap after lunch.

She rose afterward, feeling refreshed and went back to the pasture. She dug the holes and poured concrete around all the anchor posts in the new fence line. The concrete would be set before she and Ron started the next morning. It would save them a lot of time.

Later that evening, after she finished making potato salad and frying a chicken, she was more than ready for bed. She hoped she didn't oversleep and that ice cream and cookies would be okay for dessert, since she was not going to make the peach cobbler she had intended. She had wanted to do something special for that sweetheart of a guy who was going out of his way to help her repair her fence. But she was just too tired to do anything else.

The next day was pleasant with lots of sunshine and a slight south breeze. Ellen thoroughly enjoyed working with Ron. So much in fact she forgot to pursue the question of his relationship with Lila. He was a good sport and seemed to enjoy her company as well. He even said he loved ice cream and cookies. They even got a little philosophical in their conversations.

"You are so different from all the other women I know," he said rather tentatively.

"In what way?" she asked.

"Well, you chose a field that requires a lot of physical labor, and it's not really a glamorous profession."

"Don't go there," she cautioned.

"No, no. I like it. It's just kind of unusual to find a woman that doesn't think expensive possessions and 'pretty' are all that matter."

"Our society seems to measure success by how much money you make and how expensive your possessions are, but I agree with Rudyard Kipling—if you can treat triumph and disaster the same—you've won the game."

"Do you want to explain that?" he asked.

"Well, I look at life as a test. The main precept

being: know yourself and be true to that. I had a hard time with it at first, you know. Like, how is it possible to treat those two imposters just the same?"

"You mean triumph and disaster?"

"Yes, I thought…how can anyone who strives to be triumphant and successful feel the same about disaster and failure. I thought Kipling surely had a screw loose."

"I can see that for sure."

"Well, everyone strives for true happiness. Right?"

"Yeah, I think so."

"But, do we really know what true happiness is? We tend to look 'out there' for it: bigger house, a more expensive car, etc. We see 'Old Joe' in his new Bentley and he seems so happy, we think we just have to have one too. But, what we are seeing may be 'Old Joe's' *expectation* that his new Bentley will bring him happiness. Also, I think most of us confuse happiness with pleasure."

"Tell me the difference."

"I believe you will know true happiness as a deep down soul satisfaction that all is as it should be: that *you* are what you were intended to be. That does not mean you have to exclude pleasure. Enjoy. Just keep all facets of your life in harmony with your soul pattern."

"How do I know what my soul pattern is?" he asked.

"Ron, my sweet, wonderful friend." She laughed. "I don't really know how to explain it. I guess the closest I can come to it is: listen to your conscience. We seem to have forgotten we have one, what with the hustle of trying to keep up with the Joneses. I think if you can hang onto your soul harmony through triumphs and disasters, you have treated those two imposters just the same."

"I see." he said, contemplating her interpretation.

"Goodness! I didn't mean to wax philosophical on

you. I only meant to say that I love what I do, and it gives me a lot of satisfaction and helps me to know who I am—what I am capable of and what I am not. I think I am happy…well, was happy. If we could just find Bud and know that he is okay, you know. This is a disaster that I have to keep remembering could cause me to lose my soul harmony."

"What do you mean?"

"Well, I would like very much to do terrible harm to a certain person, whose name shall not be mentioned here. I think if I did that, I would cause terrible disruption of the harmony of my very being."

Ron smiled at her. "I think it will all turn out okay, and I thank you for the lesson in philosophy."

"Oh gosh, I didn't mean to get so carried away. I just don't have many people to converse with. After a moment's reflection, she laughingly continued, "Maybe that's a part of my satisfaction."

They laughed together. It was fun, this sharing of thoughts while sharing their physical labor.

First they hung the gates between the anchor posts, which closed off the gap between the two properties and kept all the bovine critters on their own home turf—except Old Rogue, of course. They took down the damaged fence just ahead of putting up the new and finished approximately one half of the fence the first day. They did not, however, finish the entire fence on the second day, but they were close. They were a few posts short and were about to call it quits, when they heard a vehicle approaching.

There, coming across the pasture, was Lila in her new bronze Cadillac. When Lila stopped and stepped out of her car, Ellen couldn't help noticing her beautiful white crepe blouse and her extremely high heels that sank at least two inches into the dirt.

"Don't guess you came out to work," Ron greeted

her, commenting on the way she was dressed.

Lila laughed, "Are you kidding? I wouldn't know where to start, and I don't want to learn. Working is for people who aren't smart enough to avoid it."

Ellen said nothing. She thought, *Wonder what she'd say if she knew that I not only don't avoid it, but get a great deal of satisfaction out of it? What she would say if she knew what I think of her because she avoids it? Oh well, different strokes for different folks.*

Ellen and Ron continued picking up their tools, and after a few moments of silence, Ellen asked, "What brings you out here, Lila?"

"I came out to get a few packs of flowers. You were not at the house, and since the property is half mine, I started to help myself, but your stupid dog doesn't know I'm entitled. He actually tried to bite me." Lila was indignant.

Ellen experienced a surge of love for Old Seizer. She laughed. "Smart dog! You do not own any part of my business, and if you take anything, I will file theft charges on you. Is that clear?"

Lila looked at Ron and appealed to him for support. "You're the law here. Tell her I'm right."

Ron looked uncomfortable, but before he could speak, Ellen's mighty-fine-neighbor drove up in his burgundy truck. Lila seemed to lose interest in everything except the confident stride of Zack's tight jeans and broad shoulders. Ellen herself drew in a deep breath at the sight of him.

As she watched Lila, she saw something that caused her hopes to rise. The buttons on Lila's beautiful crepe blouse were small circles of golden lace with clear diamond-like settings in the center. And sure enough, while the right sported two, one was missing from the cuff of her left sleeve.

Zack had seen the button at Bud's house the first

night they had met. Ellen needed a witness to vouch for this new finding. Somehow Zack had to notice those buttons! Ellen kept trying to attract Zack's attention, but to no avail. He seemed to be avoiding eye contact. He went to check out the new fence, and after tugging at the posts and strumming the wires, remarked that it was indeed well built.

Zack was helping Ron pick up and roll a few loose strands of the old fence when an end of one strand flipped and pulled a barb across Zack's ear.

"Ouch," he groaned and reached to grab his ear.

*Here was an opportunity,* Ellen thought. "Better let me wash that with peroxide and apply a band-aid," she said.

"No, that's okay. I'll take care of it when I get home."

"Sorry, I insist," Ellen replied, taking the first aid kit from her truck. "Rusty wire and all that, you know."

She saturated a paper towel with peroxide and reached up to swab Zack's ear. He moved to take the paper towel from her, but she put both her hands on the sides of his face.

He stared at her as she said, "Bend down just a little."

She put her mouth closer to his ear than was really necessary and whispered very softly, "Look at the buttons on Lila's blouse."

Zack played it very cool, as though he was an old pro at the game. He complained about the punishment she was inflicting on his ear and how much it burned. He thanked Ellen though and went on gathering the last bits of wire.

Lila couldn't resist. She slipped out of her high heels and walked up to Zack and introduced herself. Ellen noted that Zack did indeed check out her buttons.

*That and more*, she guessed. She would call him

later and see what he thought about the button evidence.

Zack offered to pay Ellen his share of the fence repair costs right then. She said they still had a few more expenditures before she would have the total figure. And, if it were okay with Ron to wait on his share and if Zack would give her his cell phone number, she would call him with the final accounting.

As they were leaving, Lila drove the fence line. She drove her Cadillac into rougher terrain than Ellen ever would have.

*Probably thinks she'll get stuck, and the guys will stay and get her out*, thought Ellen as she drove back to her house to begin her nightly tasks.

Ron waved as he drove through the yard, and Lila looked the other way when she passed. Zack stopped and knocked on Ellen's back door.

"Come in," she called. Zack entered, lightly rubbing his ear.

"Does it hurt much?" she asked. "I have some Tylenol if you'd like."

"No, it's not that bad," he said. "Just bleeding a little."

"Here, I have a better band-aid," Ellen said, returning with a gauze-padded one. She reached to replace the one on his ear. He leaned in closer. She felt the heat of him. He lifted his arms as though to embrace her. Her pulse quickened. She felt an exquisite tightness in the core of her being. She wanted this closeness. But he abruptly stiffened. Straightening and pulling away, he took the band-aid from her hand.

She felt bereft, like a child whose lollipop was jerked away just as the sweetness of it had touched the tongue. She was certain he felt the strong attraction as well. Why did he deny it? It had to be Jennifer. This was going to be hard for Ellen to handle. She would have to avoid his presence to maintain her composure.

She cleared her throat and said, "I was wondering what we should do about Lila's buttons. I mean, we will tell the sheriff of course, but what can they do?"

"There's really not much that it proves, actually," he answered. "She could say it was there from another time. Who can refute that?"

Ellen's heart sank. She was further denied. What he said was probably true, or did he just want her to drop the matter? Had he taken the matching button left on Jennifer's table? He had had the opportunity. There were so many questions and almost no answers. And who was she supposed to trust? She felt close to tears. Perhaps, she was just overly tired.

"Guess you're right. Well, I'll call you when the fence is finished."

He looked at her as Jennifer had earlier; as though he wanted to say something, but didn't.

She turned her back and walked away, saying, "I've got to feed baby, so I'll see ya." Besides, she didn't think she wanted to hear what he was going to say.

After a moment's hesitation, he replied. "Thanks a lot for taking on the fence challenge."

"No problemo. It's my fence too," she remarked as she left the room.

That night as she tried to relax and fall asleep, she felt again that momentary closeness. The sweetness of that expectation before it was suddenly snatched away. She thought he had felt it too. It hurt to know he had a prior commitment.

Tears filled her eyes. She thought, *I seem to be on the horns of a dilemma.* She chuckled. *That's mighty strange. I don't have one damn horn in my entire herd.* Disgusted with her lame attempt at humor, she chastised herself. *You're so weird! Beyond all hope!*

All did seem beyond hope. What was the use? She

relinquished the hold on her composure and gave in to an all-consuming, tearful session of questions without answers about what was really going on and just what she was supposed to do about it all.

# Chapter Seven

Ellen told herself she was simply on edge because she had overreached her energy levels for the last few days. Some time to relax was what she needed. Only she had to go and get those extra posts! She could finish the fence all by herself and she would. *Still, a few extra hours won't make too much difference*, she thought.

So she took time to give Old Seizer the biggest hug and the best rub down he'd gotten in some time.

"Just keep up the good work, old fellow," she encouraged, as he carefully took the offered sausage and biscuit reward from her hand.

After treating herself to another cup of coffee, Ellen took a leisurely hour to sit in the shade and listen to the birds in her back yard. On her way back into the house to dress for her everyday routine with the animals and the work in the greenhouses, Ellen noticed Old Yowler waiting at the patio door. Perhaps jealous of Ellen's display of affection for Old Seizer, Yowler had brought her a present. A gift of a mouse. He laid it next to the door on the back patio. It had been some time since he had brought her a mouse.

*Thank goodness for the little bit of sweet that comes with the bitter,* she thought. *At least my cat loves me.* Ellen laughed and rubbed his coat. He leaned into her, enjoying it, before going on to his bowl in the kitchen. *Do cats feel rejected, if they see you dispose of their gifts?* she wondered.

A little later than usual, she went into Malden for the extra posts. She wanted to stop by the sheriff's office, but was tired of being such a nuisance. She wanted to tell Sheriff Hewitt about Lila's statement that

71

a secret agent, called Sid, was trying to send Carlo back to Mexico. She had forgotten to pass on that information in their earlier conversation.

*I'll just call when I get home*, she thought. *I'm not sure he'll find that less intrusive, but I guess it'll take up less of his time.*

On her way home, as she topped the hill just past Bud's house, she saw a black SUV pull out of her drive and speed away.

"That's the one!" she exclaimed. "That's the one I saw blast past the house the day Bud disappeared!"

She pressed hard on the accelerator and began catching up. Evidently she was spotted. The vehicle started rapidly pulling away from her. She was determined to get the license plate number and drove even faster—too fast, she was sure—to be within the sanctions of the law.

Ellen was close on their tail for over a mile. As she was approaching a blind intersection, a burgundy truck pulled out onto the road between her and the disappearing black streak. Zack!

"Oh my God!" was her plea for help. She slammed on her brakes with all her strength. Her brakes caught and held, then released, then caught again, then released again.

"Stupid anti-lock brakes!" She frantically fought for control of her wildly careening vehicle. The premonition she had had when she first met Zack sped through her mind. Was this the ultimate disaster it foretold? Was this to be end of them both?

Zack gave her the whole road, pulling off to the side as far as possible. She had narrowly missed him and was on the wrong side of the road, partially off in a ditch, when her truck finally came to a stop. She was trembling uncontrollably. She felt completely stupid, but was extremely thankful she had not hit anyone.

She was resting her head on the steering wheel when Zack approached, asking, "Are you okay?" Thank God he was there and safe.

"Yes…yes, I think so," she managed to reply, rubbing her arm.

"That was quite an exhibition of driving skills," he said quietly. "Why were you chasing that car?"

"That was the SUV I saw the day Bud disappeared. It was just coming out of my driveway," she answered breathlessly. "I wanted the license number. They must surely be involved in Bud's disappearance. What were they doing in my driveway?"

"Did you get their license number?"

"No. No, I didn't quite get close enough," she answered.

"You really should leave the police work to the professionals," he advised her. "It can be very dangerous business."

Anger flared at his reprimand. How was this man able to make her feel so much in so many different ways?

"Don't give me that crap, you jerk! What was I supposed to do! Sit here and phone the sheriff? What good would that do? Besides, what in the holy…why did you pull out in front of me, anyway? You're the one that made it dangerous!"

His eyes held hers for a time. "You lost a couple of posts back there. If you will turn around, I'll pick them up for you."

She made no reply. Starting her truck, she hoped she would be able to back out of the ditch.

When she was finally turned around and headed back in the other direction, she saw Jennifer getting back into Zack's vehicle.

She pulled up close to where he stood. "I should have the fence finished this afternoon and will call you with the final figures," she informed him as he put the posts in her truck.

Do you really want to do all that by yourself?" he asked.

"Yes. There's not much left to do," she mumbled as she drove away. She was relieved to escape further scrutiny from those unreadable blue eyes.

After calming herself—which took a little time—Ellen had a bite of lunch and called the sheriff with the information about an agent named Sid who was trying to send Carlo back to Mexico.

"Huh! Wonder how they determined that? Must be a leak somewhere," was Sheriff Hewitt's only comment about the bit of news. "Be careful," were his last gruff words, as he hung up the phone.

*I have to do more on my own and quit bothering the sheriff's department,* she promised herself. *They don't ever know anything anyway.*

Ellen herself finished the repairs on the fence. She was clipping up the wires to the last post when Zack's truck came towards her across the pasture. *Another Rogue in my pasture without invitation. What timing! Is he psychic or was he watching through binoculars? Guess he wanted to see if my work measured up to the rest of the fence.*

Jennifer was there again in the truck with Zack. Ellen felt somewhat embarrassed—or rather rejected—because of the evening before. Zack must surely have felt those highly-charged vibes she was generating when he stood so close. Maybe not. At this moment, she hoped not.

Zack helped attach the last few strands of barbed wire while Jennifer self-consciously tried to make small talk.

Soon the fence was completely finished; then came the hard part: separating Old Rogue from the herd. Ellen had brought a bucket of cubes to entice him through the gate. If she could just keep her cows from following him, it would work.

"If you can keep him interested in the bucket of cubes at the gate, I will try to drive the rest down to the other end," she told Zack.

"Sounds good," he replied. "He should love that."

Ellen patiently circled her cows and drove them slowly away from the gate. Soon she was at the other end of the pasture, where Lila had bounced around in her Cadillac the day before.

She turned to see Zack entice Old Rogue through the gates and then fasten him out of her pasture. She had started back towards her truck when she noticed the toe of a boot sticking out of the sand. She walked over to it and tried to pick it up. It wouldn't budge. It was attached to something. A leg, Ellen realized. She screamed. Falling to her knees, she began digging the sand away from the body with her bare hands.

She was still screaming and sobbing when Zack came running up. Jennifer trailed behind.

"No! Don't. Please, Ellie don't," he pleaded.

Lifting her up and away from the body, he pulled her close to him, pressing her head into his shoulder. "It's not your brother. It's not Bud," he repeated.

The meaning of his words finally pierced her understanding, and she immediately wondered, *How do you know?*

She did not voice the question, but stepped back and watched Zack call the authorities from his cell phone. Was it her imagination or had he called her sweetheart as he tried to calm her down?

Jennifer, with tears in her eyes, put both arms around Ellen and kept saying, "I'm so sorry. I'm so sorry, Ell." She tried to get Ellen to go back to her truck, but Ellen very firmly refused.

"No! I'm stay'n," she said.

It seemed Jennifer was more concerned with Ellen's emotional state than the identity of the body still covered in sand.

Soon several cars from the County Sheriff's Department showed up. Sheriff Hewitt and Ron Brady were with them. Ron immediately went to Ellen and put his arms around her.

"Are you alright?" he asked, concern in his voice.

"It's not Bud. I don't think it's Bud. Those boots are too big, and he would never wear a pair so gaudy." Ellen pointed to the boot she had uncovered that sported a bright yellow portion above the ankle.

"Thank God for all favors," Ron said.

She assumed he meant that though they had not found Bud, at least they had not found him dead. He kissed Ellen on the cheek and hugged her again. Ellen glanced up and saw Zack look away. Did it matter to him that Ron had kissed her?

Sheriff Hewitt asked everyone to stand back a good distance so they would not disturb the crime scene. Ron asked Ellen and Jennifer if they wanted to sit with him in his cruiser until the coroner arrived. They both accepted gratefully. Ellen was completely exhausted, but determined to stay until the investigation was complete. If anything was learned that pointed to Bud's disappearance, she wanted to know the whole skinny.

Zack encouraged Jennifer to take his truck and go home to rest. He said he would bum a ride with one of the deputies.

Eventually, the coroner arrived and the body was uncovered. After a cursory exam, he told the sheriff what he had learned. "At this point, there is no way to identify the corpse. It is male and has been shot in the face and neck. There is not a scrap of identification on him and he's probably been dead a month or so, even though this site was freshly dug."

Dried clay was embedded in parts of the clothing. So, the coroner surmised the body had been buried elsewhere and recently moved. He said he would know more after the autopsy.

Ron walked Ellen to her truck and gave her a final hug. He asked if she would be alright by herself. She assured him she would be and that she was relieved to have the day end. Tomorrow she would have to ask Ron what his fee was for helping build the fence and get those figures to Zack and the payment back to Ron. At least Old Rogue was out of her pasture for good...she hoped. After some thought, she considered the fact that there had been two uninvited intruders in her pasture; albeit, one was hidden underground. She was glad both were gone. It seemed uncanny they both left the same day, almost the same hour. And what about the third rogue who had held her in his arms? *I wouldn't say he was unwelcome, but he might present the biggest problem of them all,* she cautioned herself.

She was soon in bed and fell asleep immediately. She dreamed someone was calling her sweetheart as he held her in his arms while she tried to fight her way out of a dark, engulfing tunnel.

Several days passed before Ellen learned the body she had found belonged to one Pedro Lopez. He had a record and was a known drug dealer with close ties to a Mexican drug cartel. He was suspected of being a close associate of Carlo Rodriguez. And he was, according to forensic reports, definitely the one who had lost so much blood at Bud's house the day Bud went missing.

Now maybe they were getting somewhere. Things seemed to be falling into place. Or were they? There were still too many "ifs", "whos" and "whys" in the equation to know much for sure.

Ellen knew Pedro Lopez was at Bud's on that fateful day. She knew there was a good chance that Lila was too. She knew there had to have been an altercation between Bud and Pedro or at least someone had caused them both to bleed. If Lila were there and she was as close to Carlo as she claimed, was Carlo there too? Good chance he was.

Who shot Pedro? Had Carlo? Or Lila? Surely not Bud. Ellen didn't think Bud had a pistol. She knew he had a 12 gauge Mossberg. Pedro couldn't have been shot with that though. It would have taken off his head.

What was a drug dealer doing at Bud's house anyway? Bud had absolutely nothing to do with drugs. Ellen would stake her life on it. And drug dealers would not be involved in a petty robbery. Then why were they there? Why beat him up? What did her brother have that they would want? Ellen could think of absolutely nothing drug dealers would want from Bud. That left Lila. What did Bud have that Lila would want?

Everything he had! She had already confessed that. And if Carlo liked her as much as she said, would he force Bud to sign papers or whatever else Lila wanted? Papers? What kind of papers? Divorce papers? Those had already been filed, according to what the sheriff had told her.

*Looks like it would all be in the hands of the court already,* Ellen reasoned.

But where was Bud? Had he shot Pedro somehow? Was he in hiding for fear the Mexican cartel would exact retribution? Hardly likely, since it appeared they had taken him away in their van. Had Lila been able to take him? Surely not. Not by herself at least. She had to have had help. Who liked Lila enough to help her do such a thing?

Carlo evidently. And Ron liked her…or had in the past. Did he still? Hopefully not. If Lila had come with demands for Bud, would she have brought Carlo? Who knows what Lila would do?

Ellen called Jennifer to ask if Bud had weapons other than the Mossberg.

"Did Bud own a handgun?" Ellen inquired.

"No, just the shotgun and a hunting rifle. It's here too and loaded."

"Bud himself was hurt. Do you suppose he was somehow able to take a gun away from Pedro? Probably not…not with another assailant standing by," Ellen reasoned.

"Maybe Lila shot at Bud and was such a bad shot she hit Pedro instead," Jennifer quipped.

Ellen thought there may have been some merit to the supposition.

"Well, we know Bud was hurt. He didn't have a gun unless there was some fluke of an accident that put one in his hands. And if he had shot Pedro, why didn't he shoot the other guy? Or the other guy shoot him? It looked like the other guy, maybe Carlo, had shot Pedro. If the dead guy were shot before Bud was hurt, who hurt Bud? Not Lila, surely. Then it had to have been Carlo, unless there was a third guy. Or a fourth or a fifth!

"Shoot, all this speculation is getting us nowhere!" Ellen cried dejectedly. "Anyway you look at it, Carlo seems to be the shooter. But we're still holding an empty bag. As far as proof goes, we have none. I so wish Bud were here." Ellen needed consoling.

Jennifer wanted to help. "I feel very positive about all of this, Ell. Please don't try so hard. The sheriff and …," she hesitated, then continued, "his deputies will surely find out who did this, and I'm certain Bud is somewhere safe. I know it will all turn out well. It has to. You're killing yourself with all this worry, and I don't think we'll come up with anything significant anyway."

This was a switch. Ordinarily, Ellen was consoling Jennifer. And how was it that she felt so certain Bud was safe?

*Just words to console me,* Ellen told herself.

Oh, Lord! Who would know what really happened? Probably only three people: Bud, Lila and most likely Carlo. How to get the answers from them was the big question. Bud couldn't be found. Ellen did not know Carlo—and didn't want to—unless it became the last avenue of hope. It appeared to Ellen that Lila had to be the only source of information, at least the most likely to reveal Bud's whereabouts. If she knew. Since she seemed to be snooping around for information, maybe Lila didn't know where Bud was either.

Spending time with Lila for whatever reason would be a most disagreeable task for Ellen, but someone had to find answers and no one else was standing in line to do it?

Then, Ellen remembered what Sheriff Hewitt had said about the information Ellen had given him earlier. "Must be a leak somewhere," he had said. Meaning someone in law enforcement was passing on information to the drug cartel. Who did Ellen know that was connected to both? Lila was somewhat connected to the cartel, and she was somewhat connected to law enforcement...through Ron Brady.

*No! It could not be Ron!* Ellen rejected the notion. *He was too nice a guy.*

But was he being nice to her for spurious reasons? Perhaps to help Lila garner information about Bud and his business? If he were the leak, surely it had to have been unintentional. Yet he seemed to be a really sharp guy. Ellen couldn't imagine he would slip up and divulge key information accidentally. No, it had to be someone other than Ron. Who else in the sheriff's department had dated Lila?

Ellen admittedly didn't know many of the deputies. Perhaps she should spend a little extra time in the sheriff's office and get to know more about the people who enforced the law—and those who didn't.

# Chapter Eight

Stuck in a quandary, wondering which way to jump, Ellen let her mind wander back to the time it all started.

Zack was tight on the heels of those in the black SUV. Was he with them? One of them? How had he known that the body of Pedro Lopez was not that of Bud's before it was uncovered? He had, also, cut her off from getting the license plate number of the SUV. Had he also taken the gold lace button to destroy evidence?

The thought of his possible guilt made Ellen physically ill. That just couldn't be. It had to be wrong. *Oh, Lord, please don't let that be true!*

Why was he spending so much time with Jennifer and how had it happened so suddenly? Had they known each other before? Was that why he bought property nearby? Was the baby Jen was carrying really his, not Bud's? If so, why keep it a secret? No! It could not be true.

"Good Lord! I'm really getting so paranoid, I'd suspect my own mother!" Ellen critically chastised herself.

The idea was absolutely preposterous. Jen was too fine a person not to be up-front about a thing like that. She even felt Zack was too. But con artists knew how to make you trust them, she admitted.

She had to have some answers. Maybe background checks would shed some light on who Zack was, where he had come from and how he had earned his livelihood in the past. Checking out Ron might be useful too. Might as well check out Carlo Rodriguez also. Their paths may have crossed somewhere.

Ellen wished she were more Internet savvy. She needed some schooling in that area. But she needed answers now! Sandy! Sandy was the answer. She was librarian at the Malden library. She was also a whiz on the computer… and the Internet as well.

She and Sandy had been best friends before Ellen married Harry. Ellen had gotten so busy trying to go to college and be a perfect wife that she and Sandy had drifted apart. After the Harry-Lila fiasco, Ellen pretty much cut herself off from everyone. Now, she would see if Sandy could help.

When Sandy answered the phone, she seemed delighted that Ellen had called.

"Hey, Sandy, This is Ell. How've you been?"

"Gracious me! Ellen Wade! What a wonderful surprise! I'm fine. It's so good to hear from you."

After several minutes of filling in the time gap that had separated them, Ellen asked, "Sandy, I wonder if I could impose on your net expertise to gather some info?"

"Of course, Ell, I would love to help if I can. What specifically do you need?"

"Could I just come by at your convenience and talk with you about it?"

"Sure can. I take a break at 10:00 every morning at the library or come see me after 4:00 at my house. Better call first if you drop by my house."

"I'll be in town Monday morning. Is that okay?"

"Sure, 10:00 on Monday morning, then."

Early on Monday morning, Ellen bought apple fritters and doughnuts. Then she went by the sheriff's office to get a quote from Ron on his price for helping with her fence. She normally would have done that before building the fence, but she had known Ron would be reasonable. If not, she would take up the slack herself; working with him had been worth the full price.

She was hoping to gain a little rapport with some of

the deputies by bringing a variety of doughnuts. It seemed to have worked. All three deputies in the office at that time thanked her graciously, offered her coffee and made a few jokes. One even said laughingly, "Come back and see us any time; we love doughnuts." None looked like a criminal. The sheriff had no new information concerning Bud.

"You still have nothing more on the persons of interest you mentioned last week?" she asked.

"No. Detective work is hard work, and it takes a lot of time," replied Sheriff Hewitt, tugging on his graying mustache. "And we have to be 'specially careful with all the evidence. I understand you're worried about your brother, but we can't manufacture evidence." He reached in his breast pocket for his small pipe.

Ellen apologized for bothering him again and hurried to the library to discuss her problem with Sandy.

Sandy hadn't changed much, except her long blond hair was now in a soft fluffy bob, and the mole on her chin had been removed. She was delighted to see Ellen, and she expressed sympathy over Bud's disappearance.

"I'm so sorry to hear that Bud is missing. He was such a great guy."

"*Is* a great guy! We've not given up—we have to find him. I won't go into detail about all that happened. There are just some questions in my mind that need answers, and I need to satisfy my curiosity about a few people who may or may not be connected to the disappearance."

She asked Sandy to be discreet and not mention Ellen's interest in the three persons she wanted to know more about.

"Of course, Ell, I'll not say a word."

Ellen knew she wouldn't. "Thanks. I need all the info you can find on Zack Cunningham, Ron Brady and Carlo Rodriguez."

Sandy told Ellen that she knew Ron well. "Oh, my. I don't have to look *him* up. I know all about him...well, not as much as I would like to know. We both grew up in the next county. He was a rather rambunctious teenager, but a good kid, and turned out to be a 'peach of a guy.'"She knew there would be nothing bad on his record. "I've never heard of the other two," she said.

But she promised to get on the Internet and Google or check criminal histories and ancestries or whatever she could think of. She promised to call Ellen soon. Ellen felt an indebtedness and real sorrow that she had let their friendship lapse. She would rectify that.

With that source of information in the works, Ellen considered how to learn about Lila's intentions—in detail if possible. Lila liked to drink and she also liked to talk. Maybe there was a way. Ellen went by the liquor store and bought various bottles of alcoholic beverages, including tequila, vodka and several bottles of wine. Lila could take her pick. Ellen started to buy a bottle of her own favorite, Barringer's White Zinfandel. But at the last minute she thought better of it. She liked it too much. The objective was to get Lila to drink, not to drink herself.

Ellen knew she could not make overtures of friendship towards Lila. Lila would be immediately suspicious, so Ellen had to wait until Lila came to her.

Meanwhile, she was also waiting to get some answers from her attorney. Ellen wasn't a person who liked to wait. She needed to be busy. So she was glad to discover her hay meadows were ready for their first cutting. She had learned the best way to deal with grief was to work until you dropped, then one could "*lie in the arms of Morpheus*" and be completely oblivious to it all.

Ellen cut only one meadow at a time with her

swather. The swather squeezed the juices out of the grass, letting it cure faster. Cutting one field at a time allowed her to barn all her hay sooner; all her bales were picked up quickly. Sometimes, picking up bales as soon as they hit the ground was critical when it was thundering, and sprinkles of rain were already dampening your cheeks. She watched the weather forecasts continuously before and during haying season.

Ellen loved the smell of freshly mown hay. It had a fresh clean, delicate scent all its own. The fields looked beautiful to her as well, everything cut smoothly with no scraggly weeds to spoil the golf course look of them.

After the field was cut, the hay would cure for a day or so and then be turned or actually flipped, so the bottom of the row would cure properly as well. It was important to get the curing time just right; it made a great difference in quality of the hay.

While the hay cured, Ellen worked in her garden. A few green beans were ready to harvest. She wanted a few new potatoes to serve with the fresh green beans and buttered cornbread; so she dug under one side of a potato plant and stole some small potatoes. The mother vine never knew, or didn't care. There would be no serious fallout, much like an old mother hen on a nest. She might squawk a little if one lifted her up to check the progress of her incubation prowess. But she would settle back on the nest, clucking softly, nurturing the rest of the brood through the maturation process.

Squash to fill the freezer and to make relish was now ready in abundance. There would be a goodly amount to sell at the farmers' market, as well. Beets were ready for pickling. Ellen usually pickled beets one year and cucumbers the next. It saved on labor and she always had plenty of each in her cellar. And with the price of pickles being what they were, it was well worth the effort. Ellen liked her ice box pickles the best.

After a few days, the hay in the first meadow was ready to bale. It had cured perfectly and would be excellent hay. Ellen started hauling bales late in the day after all the grass was baled. She worked late into the night to finish, using the lights on her truck, since there was no bright moon.

It could get very hot stacking in the barns, so she appreciated the cool night air.

Old Seizer was always right there behind Ellen as she tediously loaded hay, bale after bale onto her truck. She liked the small bales since her fields weren't really large enough to warrant larger equipment and bigger bales. She did have a hay loader, but didn't use it at night. She didn't like pulling a trailer when she couldn't see everything clearly.

Old Seizer was loyal and protective, and Ellen loved his company in the fields after dark. But she wished he would give up one of his most curious habits. After trying to discern just why he did such an unusual thing, Ellen could only suppose that he thought the objective of all the haying business was to completely clear the fields and leave no litter, nothing whatsoever, behind. So when he felt the urge, in order to not leave any unwanted feces on the cleanly raked and cleared field, Old Seizer would climb upon a bale of hay and do his thing.

Ellen usually had to leave two or three bales in the fields because of it. But his company was worth the cost.

At last it was time to see James Caldwell, the attorney. Ellen had a rather long list of questions to ask and hoped some of the answers would relieve her apprehension.

Caldwell's office bespoke success. The rather expensive leather furniture was comfortable as well as beautiful. There were quite a number of green plants; well cared for, green and growing. Ellen appreciated that. She detected the aroma of a sweet-smelling pipe tobacco. She thought it was beechnut or something like that. But it was definitely the same pipe tobacco her father had always smoked.

James Caldwell was an older man with graying temples. *Good,* thought Ellen, *lots of experience.*

He was dressed impeccably, and his bearing signified complete competence. It was confidence inspiring. Pleasant and courteous, he was intent upon helping Ellen with her problems.

Ellen didn't know exactly how much she should divulge of what she suspected but could not prove. The best course of action, she decided, was to tell only the facts and let him come up with his own assessments…or suspicions.

She felt as if she had met him before. She had. He was the elderly gentleman who had asked her to dance at the Country Club the night Lila had commanded Ron to dance with her.

Anxiously, Ellen asked her most pressing question. "Well, to start with, my brother is missing and his wife—he thought they were divorced—is trying to take all he has once more. Can she do that while he is missing and unable to defend himself?"

The attorney answered her directly without any hard to understand legal mumbo-jumbo. "If the court cannot serve Bud with divorce papers, she will have to wait the statutory time limit before the court can grant her a divorce. In Oklahoma the time limit is five years," he informed her.

Ellen breathed a sigh of relief. At least there was some time.

"What if he has been killed?" she asked.

"Well, if they are indeed still married, and he has no

other relative as close or closer, like a child, she would inherit it all."

A red flag went up in Ellen's mind. Jen and her baby could be in jeopardy. Maybe Zack *was* trying to protect her.

"Well, Lila took, or Bud gave her, everything he had when they divorced—when he thought they had divorced. They have not lived together since, and most of what he has now, he inherited from our parents. I don't think he has even spoken to her since," Ellen replied. "Can she take all that from him as well?"

"If she told him she had divorced him, and he had signed the papers, there being no cohabitation afterwards; and if he had not included her in any of his holdings in any way, that would have a great impact on the court in his favor," he told her. "Also, a spouse cannot take any part of an inheritance if that inheritance was held intact or separate from his other assets. That means all that Bud inherited from his parents is his. She cannot take any part of it from him. But he cannot mix any of those assets with other funds that they jointly held."

Ellen wondered if Bud had commingled his earnings with his inherited monies. Chances are he had.

"Was there an insurance policy?"

It was a question Ellen had never considered.

"I don't know," she replied. "I will ask Jennifer to go through his belongings. If there is a policy, maybe we can find it. Can Lila interfere in my business because Bud and I became partners?" Ellen asked.

"I suppose that might happen. If there is no record of a divorce and she is still his wife, she should be able to petition the court to run his/her one half of the business."

Ellen's heart sank. How could this be happening to her?

After a brief hesitation, he asked, "Did he pay you cash for his half of the business?"

"No, he had just bought his property out near me and wanted a little time to get the money for the business together."

"Did you have a contract?"

"Yes, even though I really hadn't wanted one."

"Always want one. Get it all in writing. Though he was your brother and very trust-worthy, you see here why circumstances can force issues. Does the contract specify any action in case of default?"

"Yes, I think he loses all claim after missing three payments."

"And how many payments has he missed?"

James Caldwell must be a really good attorney, Ellen thought. He was pointing out some very pertinent details that had never occurred to her.

"Two. He has missed two payments so far," she said.

"Well, let's just be very quiet about this whole thing and the minute he has missed that third payment, we'll file papers to put all his business interest back in your name."

"But if he's not here to contest it, will it work?" Ellen asked.

"Probably not, but we can tie it up in court until the case is settled about whether or not she's really his wife. It depends a lot on the judge, but it's worth a try. The objective here is to keep her away from you, and maybe Bud will show up before she has a right to be on your property. If she ever gets that right," he replied.

He was giving her a small ray of hope. She expressed her gratitude for his help as she rose to leave.

"That's what I'm here for. And I knew your dad, so I have sort of an added incentive," he told her.

Excitedly, she questioned, "You knew my parents?"

"Yes, your dad and I were classmates in college during our first two years. I went into law, and he chose petroleum engineering, but our paths crossed often. He was a fine man, and I liked him a lot. I was very sorry to hear about your brother's disappearance, and it was a grievous tragedy…the death of your parents. I hope you have much better luck in the future. I'd say you have already had enough disastrous misfortune."

"Mom and dad had a really tough time in the beginning, but he was determined to get that PE degree, even with two small children to support. But they persisted and after he was hired by Gulf Oil, everything went great until the tornado."

"He was very dedicated and an excellent student. I was honored to be his friend."

"I'm so pleased you knew my father. It's almost like finding a new family member," she told Attorney Caldwell as she shook his hand before leaving. Ellen hoped they would become good friends.

When Ellen did her usual work after getting home that evening, she noted Old Seizer was nowhere to be found. But she had fed her livestock a little earlier than usual and expected he would be home shortly. Picking up a bucket of cubes, she drove to the far end of her property to feed and count some yearling bulls she intended to sell. She always counted her cows daily. If one jumped the fence, it could be in the next county in twenty-four hours. Better to catch them as soon as possible. It was easy to count them all if she called them to the feed bucket first.

They came running, bucking and kicking, flinging their tails in the air. Some making loud, rude noises. Ellen called a few times anyway, just to make sure they all knew it was suppertime. As she called, she heard an answering bark across the road. She went on with her

91

counting for a few seconds before it dawned on her that
the dog barking was Old Seizer. When she finished
with the herd duties, she started across the road. Seizer
answered her every call.

After walking approximately two hundred feet,
Ellen came to a small ravine, and there in the bottom
was Old Seizer caught in traps, one trap on each of his
four feet. Underneath him lay a large heap of pork or
beef offal. It had been an irresistible enticement for
him. The traps had been strategically placed to catch at
least one foot or another of a hungry coyote. Probably,
some farmer had recently butchered for his own freezer
and had used the intestines to lure and catch a few
coyotes.

Coyotes were admittedly a great nuisance. They
would not only eat your chickens and cantaloupes out
of the garden, but kill your dog as well. It was not
uncommon for the female coyote, while she was in
heat, to lure a domestic dog away from the farmhouse,
and, during or after copulation, many other coyotes
would attack and kill the dog. Based on these incidents,
there were increasing numbers of bigger coyotes, or
coydogs as they were called, that were fathered by the
larger farm dogs. The coydogs were not only larger, but
much less afraid of humans. They were, therefore, a
much greater threat to farm animals.

Who would have used that ravine to set the traps? It
was city property, and traps were illegal there anyway,
at least without proper notification and postings that
they were set in the area.

Old Seizer was glad to see Ellen. He whimpered
and barked, even howled twice, as she descended into
the ravine. Being vigilant to avoid any additional traps,
Ellen carefully stepped on the backside of each trap
until it opened and released Old Seizer's foot. He didn't
seem able to remove his feet by himself, so Ellen

cautiously pulled each foot, one by one, from the traps. He was in considerable pain, as evidenced by the whining and biting of Ellen's hands and wrists. He was very gentle though, and the bites were tempered by a generous amount of gratitude. When he was free, he licked her face with several wet swipes and hobbled away for a good distance before hitting his stride, but continued walking with a limp. Ellen wondered how long he had been in the traps. It had to have been excruciatingly painful and probably fearful. He had several bloody marks on his face and chest. Perhaps, he had fended off a pack of coyotes. Would there eventually be coydogs large enough to kill dogs like Old Seizer, one on one?

Ellen was extremely angry because of the danger to all family pets in the area. Any trappers were legally bound to have permits to trap and to post all areas affected. Ellen had not been notified and had seen no postings. Since the land belonged to the city, it would in all probability be difficult to determine who was responsible. She didn't want traps set there again, even if Old Seizer had learned his lesson and would never again approach the ravine. Ellen decided to take the traps so they *could not* be set again. She would make as many phone calls as necessary and determine to whom they belonged.

After several phone calls, she came to a dead end. She decided to hang the traps from the arch of her front gate, noticeable to all passers-by. Perhaps the owner would call her and they could discuss the matter. Or perhaps they would just take the traps. That would be okay with Ellen, as long as they got the message loud and clear. *Do not set your traps here!*

Old Seizer was rather inactive for a time, but was then back to his usual self. No one came by, removed the traps or called about them. After a week or so had passed, Ellen was startled awake by a gunshot and a painful cry from Seizer. It was in the middle of the night and Ellen was somewhat disoriented. Not quite sure if she had really heard a gunshot, she hurriedly ran outside to see what had happened. She saw taillights disappear from sight over the hill. Were they the people in the SUV? And what had happened to Seizer? He had to have been hit; his cry had told her that.

Her nightgown flapping, she ran to her truck and drove down the lane to the road. There on the side of the driveway lay Seizer whining, his legs pawing the air as if to run away. He had been shot, point-blank in the head. Ellen hurriedly tried to lift him into her truck. She must get him to a vet immediately. But she knew before he was completely in the truck he hadn't made it.

Ellen wept shamelessly. He was a beautiful dog. A wonderful pet and yes, as trite as it sounded, a beloved member of her family. She loved that old dog. Who would have done such a senseless thing? Ellen drove to the house. She would bury him tomorrow. Knowing she would not be able to sleep, Ellen made a pot of coffee and sat in the recliner, letting her mind embrace all the wonderful memories she had of Old Seizer.

One of the most recent things he had done that had absolutely delighted her was his stand against Lila when she had tried to take "free" flowers from the greenhouse. Did Lila hate him so much that she had shot him? It didn't seem plausible to Ellen. If she had wanted him dead, she would probably have killed him sooner. The incident had happened some time ago; surely she would have calmed down by now.

Ellen remembered how he had been caught in traps not more than a week before. How he had licked her face in appreciation as she had released him.

Slowly, realization came to her that the people who

had set the traps were most likely the ones who had shot Seizer. They were angry because she had taken the traps. They certainly must have seen them hanging from the arch over her gate. She had been the cause of his death as surely as if she had pulled the trigger herself. Again she wept, overwhelmed with guilt and self-censure. Why had she not left the darn things where she had found them? They were useless to her. She hadn't wanted them. She had only wanted to confront those who had hurt Seizer in the first place. Now she had caused them to kill him. Were they such cowards they could not come forward and discuss a controversy face-to-face? Why didn't they just take their stupid traps? It was gut-wrenching. How could she ever forgive herself?

The next day Ellen removed the traps and took them back to the ravine where she had found them.

After a few dismal days, Ron called and asked if Ellen would accompany him to dinner and a movie.

"Yes." was her immediate reply. "I desperately need a diversion."

During dinner, Ron asked, "May I ask what the desperation was in your need for a diversion? Has something turned up about Bud?"

"No, it was not about Bud this time." She reluctantly told her story, admitting her culpability in taking the traps. Ron was sympathetic and told her he would see if he could determine who had set the traps.

"There's probably not much we can go on, but I will see what I can find," he promised.

"Thanks," Ellen replied with tears in her eyes. "I was told you were a peach of a guy and you really are."

He grinned. "By whom?" he asked.

"By someone who likes you a lot," she smiled.

"She's pretty and blonde and works at the library."

The next day at approximately noon, a van marked "Malden Pet Shop" pulled up to her back door. There was a knock, and when Ellen answered, she found a skinny, young man struggling to hold a very wiggly half-grown pup.

"Morning, ma'am," he greeted her.

"Good morning. You must have the wrong address," she replied.

"Ms. Ellen Wade?" he questioned.

"Yes, but...."

"Delivery of one male pup, Rottweiler-Great Dane cross to Ms. Ellen Wade.

*But from whom?* Ellen wondered, *Could those who had killed Seizer have a guilty conscience?*

"From one Ron Brady, Deputy Sheriff," finished the young delivery boy.

Ellen's heart overflowed with gratitude for Ron. He was not only a peach of a guy, but also as sweet as a sugarplum.

"Thank you so much," breathed Ellen. "Just set him down and let him make himself at home." *He may tinkle on the floor,* she thought. *But I really don't care if it makes him happy. I'll look after him.*

*What to name him?* she wondered. She laughed when *Deputy Dog* came to mind.

*Oh, just call him Brady,* she finally decided. She would only call him Deputy Dog when the other deputy was around.

# Chapter 9

Ellen was somewhat resentful of Jennifer because of her constant association with Zack. Nothing could be gained, however, by alienating her. Jennifer was carrying Bud's child, a child Ellen wanted very much to know and watch grow.

Since she was Bud's closest relative at the time, Ellen felt she had a right to insist on a key to his house. She needed to find old records that might somehow give them a clue about Bud's aggressors. But instead of pushing herself into Bud's business, Ellen asked Jennifer if she would look for any outdated insurance policies and offered to help her search for them.

"I'm sure Bud would not be paying for any insurance policy with Lila as beneficiary," Jennifer remarked.

"That was my first thought too; however, I wonder if the policy could still be in effect with Lila somehow making the payments."

"Can she do that?"

"If she's still his wife, I suppose it would not be questioned. After all, wives usually send in the checks, don't they? I'll bet they had a joint checking account," was Ellen's guess. "Wonder if he ever closed that account?"

They agreed to meet that afternoon and go through Bud's stuff. It gave Ellen a few free hours to figure out how to handle her new waggy-tailed acquisition, Brady.

Feeling the need for professional help in learning how to control her little wet-nosed pooch, Ellen went into Malden and purchased a dog-training guide for beginners. She had no experience instructing dogs, but the book gave her confidence. It was written by two women who had done it for twenty-five years.

After gathering a few groceries, she added several items for her new friend: dog food for growing puppies, tick-off, a collar, leash, brush, bedding and doggie treats. The bill was considerably higher.

*Goodness gracious,* she thought, *Old Seizer and I just sort of grew up together. I never needed a leash or a collar, not even a bed. Seizer had always slept on hay in the barn or on the mat at the back door or just on the grass under a tree in the yard.*

A feeling of doubt crept in. Had she been a proper dog owner? She knew Seizer had been a happy dog. He was healthy, and they had gotten along together superbly well. She hoped she and Brady would share the same camaraderie. She would soon be home to give him his first lesson.

Upon entering her back door, Ellen heard a sharp bark. She had shut Brady in the utility room for fear he would chew everything in sight while she was gone. Normally her pets did not stay in the house, but Brady was still a puppy and had not yet learned his territorial boundaries.

When she opened the door, Brady came bounding towards her. He had spilled the water from his bowl and slipped as he ran through it. He slid on his rump and stopped just in front of her. Laughing, she set her packages on the washing machine and bent to pick him up.

*Whoa, no, that wasn't the proper thing to do.*

She had read a portion of the first chapter in the new book, while waiting at a railroad crossing for the train to pass.

She reached for a towel, dried off her dog and wiped up the floor. Brady was jumping up and down, and all over Ellen's white pants.

She squatted to his level, firmly saying, "No."

When he settled down a bit, she rubbed his coat and told him what a good boy he was. They went through the ritual several times before Ellen stood and walked away. She thought she would like this dog fine. Perhaps she could spend some real quality time with him now that her spring rush had slackened. For now, though, she had a pressing appointment with Jennifer.

Ellen left a few minutes early and pulled into Bud's driveway as Jennifer was walking up the steps.

*She doesn't even stay here anymore, I guess. I probably wouldn't either. Too many memories and the last of them were devastating.* Ellen tried to considered things from Jennifer's point of view.

Jennifer was beginning to show a rounded tummy. It gave Ellen a jolt of happiness. She prayed with all her heart Bud was still alive. But if not, this little tyke Jennifer was carrying was the only real thing of Bud's that Ellen could hold on to, could love and help care for.

"Hey, Jen, How've you been?"

"Good...pretty good...under the circumstances."

Her eyes finally met Ellen's. There was something there, trying to express itself. Was it guilt, sorrow or what? It seemed to be concern...concern for Ellen rather than for herself...or Bud.

"I have soft drinks or would you prefer tea?" she asked Ellen.

"Tea, if you don't mind."

"Not at all. I like it better myself."

Jennifer knew right where to go to get Bud's papers. Ellen followed her into the spare bedroom Bud used for an office. There in the back of a closet were several boxes, sealed and neatly stacked. Contents were written on labels and pasted on the side of each box. It seemed Jennifer didn't need to read the labels. She set the top two or three aside. Lifting the bottom box, she carried it into the kitchen and placed it on the table.

After she finished preparing tea and pouring each of them a glass, Jennifer got a knife and opened the sealed box. Ellen had restrained herself. She could hardly wait to find something that proved Lila had an even bigger motive than just taking Bud's half of her business.

Jennifer took stacks of papers, putting some in front of Ellen. She helped herself to several other stacks.

"I'm sure Bud did have Lila as beneficiary on an insurance policy, but what does it prove one way or the other? It definitely would have lapsed by now."

"I don't know, Jen. I'm just grabbing at straws. If we find a policy, we can at least ask the insurance company if it's still in force."

"They probably won't tell us anything because we're not involved. We aren't the person who would get the money, nor the one who paid for the policy."

Jennifer was probably right. Ellen would have to find some way, though, to get that information. And a good start was the policy number or just the proof that one had existed.

After opening several envelopes that had looked promising, they were almost to the bottom of the box, when Ellen excitedly said, "Here! Here it is. Look! It's in the amount of $300,000—not a paltry sum—and Lila would get it all. You'd expect a notice of cancellation if it had lapsed, wouldn't you?"

"Yeah, you sure would. I'll check for another box— maybe later stuff." Jennifer seemed more interested now.

"And bring that box of cancelled checks," Ellen called after her. "Maybe they'll tell us something."

Nothing else was found that indicated a cancellation or lapse of the policy. After going through the box of cancelled checks, they learned there *had* been a joint account for Bud and Lila. It appeared that neither Bud nor Lila had written any checks after the date of their divorce.

"I guess he just walked off and left her the balance of over two thousand dollars," Ellen surmised. "There's no final closing statement either. If he left it to Lila, the statements would have gone to her, not to him. That is, if she had changed the address." Did she change Bud's address too? Of course.

"Right. I see where you're going with this. How do we find out if this account is still open?"

"Let's write a check and see if it bounces," Ellen answered. Smiling at the incredulous look on Jennifer's face, she continued, "No, Jen, there is a better way. Do you have a phone book?"

"Sure, but the bank won't give us her information. They'll ask for the last four digits of her social security number and we don't know what they are."

"Well," sighed Ellen, "when I get a check for a large order of plants, I find out for sure if it's good before I deliver, so this should work."

Ellen dialed the number of Fidelity Bank and Trust.

"Hi, I'm Betty Archer with Archer furniture, and I have a check here from a Robert Wade in the amount of $217.42. Can you tell me if it will be covered?"

Ellen smiled at Jennifer's raised eyebrows.

When asked, Ellen gave the bank employee the account numbers on the check and added, "It's a joint account in the names of Robert and Lila Wade." Listening for a short time, the thumb and forefinger on Ellen's free hand formed a zero as she raised it in a triumphant gesture, before saying, "Thank you very much," and hanging up.

"Yes! Yes! We were right—the account is still active."

She sobered at the thought of what the new information might mean. Could Bud be responsible for an overdraft or bad checks? "That witch is really capable of every heinous crime in the book. We gotta make sure she doesn't get away with this."

They repacked all the boxes, withholding only one bank statement and the insurance policy. After stacking the boxes back in the closet, they sat at the table discussing what all it could mean and what they could do about it.

"We know she kept the account open, which is her right. So where does that leave us?"asked Jennifer.

"Well, she has a right to keep the account in her name. Not Bud's." As an afterthought, Ellen added, "Unless they're really still married. Or she has his permission. But we have to know if the insurance policy is still in force," Ellen concluded. "Just maybe we can find out."

Ellen took the old number off of the Globe Life statement and dialed the phone.

"Yes, hello. I'm Lila Wade and I need some information on a policy concerning my missing husband, Robert Wade."

Ellen saw Jennifer's hand cover her mouth.

After a transfer to the correct person, Ellen continued, "My husband, Robert Wade, has been missing for several weeks now, and I was wondering how long I have to wait before I can claim his insurance. It was for $300,000."

She was asked for his social security number and the policy number, which Ellen gave them.

Jennifer was watching Ellen's face and soon realized she was getting information that upset her.

"Uh…yes, I know, but I wasn't sure about the length of time you had given me. Sorry to bother you again. Thank you very much."

After hanging up the phone, Ellen closed her eyes and was holding her head with both hands.

"What? What did you find out?" Jennifer needed to know.

Ellen opened her tear-filled eyes. Her voice cracked. She struggled to control herself.

"That scheming witch! That horrendous bitch!" she cried. "She's trying to kill my brother! She has to be! She *is* behind all this, and she has to pay for it...in spades!"

She burst into tears as Jennifer rushed to put her arms around her, asking, "What? What did you find out?"

Ellen wiped her cheeks. Taking a deep breath, she spoke through clenched teeth, "That useless piece of crap has maintained the policy in force and has recently increased the amount to $500,000, instead of the original $300,000. Motive aplenty, don't you think?"

"Yes...Yes." Jennifer was speechless.

"And on top of it all, she checked last week to see how long she would have to wait, if Bud is never found. Does Lila know Bud is dead or is she just hoping for an assumption of that after enough time has passed without evidence of his death?"

After a short time, Ellen, still with tears in her eyes said, "Jen, you're carrying Bud's baby. If she and her cohorts find out that bit of information, you are both in danger. You need to leave here and get some protection. She may be the sole beneficiary of his insurance, but not necessarily all his other holdings.

"Yes, I know," Jennifer answered.

Ellen hurried on, "If Bud's still alive, he needs to cancel that policy. We need to find him. Oh, God, and soon, she cried. If Lila received a cancellation notice on the insurance, she would have no motive to kill him. Maybe she and her scheming friends would back off."

"But she would know for sure that he is still alive. She might still do it out of revenge," Jennifer concluded.

Going over the facts they had just learned, Ellen rather vindictively remarked, "We should find someone to impersonate Bud and change the beneficiary on the policy to Jennifer Phillips. Then we could send Lila a thank you note for keeping it in force all these years." Hesitating, she continued, "and he ought to take all the proceeds out of that joint account too." An afterthought occurred. "That would bring revenge down on your head for sure though, wouldn't it?...No...not unless Bud is already dead. But not if *she* died first. It shouldn't change the policy if the beneficiary died, only if the insured died first."

"Why? Are you thinking of doing her in?"

"No, of course not, but she has dangerous associates. If something happened to her first, who would get the money? Bud would have to designate a new beneficiary. If he failed to do so and something happened to him, looks like his estate would inherit it. His closest relative should be able to rename the beneficiary. We need to check with Mr. Caldwell on that. We will ask him if and when it becomes necessary."

Ellen wished she could think of some way to change the recipient of all those dollars. Bud's wife and baby should be taken care of if he were not alive.

They washed and put away their glasses and Ellen started to leave.

She picked up Bud's cancelled checks and insurance papers, saying, "We'll take these in tomorrow and tell Sheriff Hewitt what we've found."

Jennifer apologetically asked, "Thanks, uh...but I...uh, would you trust me to do that, Ell? I need to talk to the sheriff anyway."

Ellen hesitated. This was a switch for Jennifer.

"I need to see the doctor too, and they'll be running all sorts of tests so it'll take the better part of the day.

104

I'm sure you won't want to wait around. I'll let you know what the sheriff advises."

Ellen knew a stall when she heard one. But she chose not to confront Jennifer, "Let me know what the doctor says too, okay?"

As Ellen drove home, she wondered about several things Jennifer had said. First, why go alone to see the sheriff? Ellen could ask Jennifer's questions of the sheriff. And she could do that while Jennifer saw the doctor. Second, what had she meant by saying, "Yes, I know," when Ellen had said her life and that of her baby's were in danger? It seemed as though she already knew their lives were in peril.

*Oh, what tangled webs we weave...*thought Ellen.

As she wearily walked toward her house, she saw Old Yowler and Miss Muffy waiting patiently by the patio door and heard an exuberantly barking Brady. She heard an engine and, as she turned, saw a burgundy truck pass her driveway going in the direction of Bud's house.

*Old Rogue was invading someone else's pasture again!*

# Chapter 10

Old Yowler and Miss Muffy were already waiting at the back door when Ellen gathered her wits about her and climbed out of bed.

She had prepared for the confrontation that was about to happen. She had purchased a cage large enough for Brady and set it in the den where he and the kitties could see each other. Brady was put in his cage with a few treats—not a large bowl of his food because he would surely spill it. Ellen talked to him for a few minutes. Then she opened the door and got down on the floor to welcome her purring felines.

Old Yowler immediately sensed a dog in the house. His back bowed up. His hair stood on end. He looked two inches taller. Miss Muffy ran behind the couch. Brady was barking and bounding around in his limited space.

Ellen firmly said "No," and for a short time, he seemed to be considering that. But he was soon barking again. Ellen turned her back and ignored him. Instead, she tried to pet Old Yowler. He went to the other side of the room. Ellen brought his food and sat on the floor between him and the caged adversary. Soon Old Yowler was eating, but warily peeking around her at the still bouncing canine in the cage.

Ellen went on about her business. Before long Brady stopped barking, and Miss Muffy eventually joined Old Yowler. After they finished their breakfast, Ellen opened the door and they fled. Miss Muffy went up the closest pecan tree, and Old Yowler headed for the barn.

It would take some time for them to understand Brady would not hurt them. She had to convince Brady that they were a part of the family and not intruders. And the cats had to believe in the serene family scene, as well. They could not run from Brady.

Ellen sighed. *Could that really happen? The "how to" book said so.*

After her other chores were done, Ellen gathered produce from her garden. Green onions and radishes were plentiful. She also picked generous amounts of lettuce, kale and Swiss chard. She never sold greens and she always had more than she could use. She would take some to Jennifer.

As Ellen washed her garden bounty, the phone rang. Sandy was on the line. She had found almost no information about the three people Ellen had asked her to check out on the Internet.

"Hi, Ell. Sorry I haven't called sooner, but I found no information on a Zack Cunningham and not much on Rodriguez. I kept looking... thinking there had to be something somewhere."

"Nothing? Nothing at all on Zack? How can that be?"

"Well, he may be in the system under another name. You know...maybe instead of Zachary Cunningham, it might be William Z. Cunningham. Who knows? I found two Zachary Cunninghams, but they were not the right age and neither had ever lived in Oklahoma. As for Rodriguez, he showed up about five years ago. Must have been in Mexico or somewhere else before that. He has several charges on his police record: possession of small amounts of cocaine, meth or weed. Also has two assault charges. Owns a horse ranch—rather nice one south of Amber City. Wonder how he got the money? Maybe he's running drugs. He probably has a lot of help and his help takes the risk. I would guess that's why there are no more serious charges. They take the risk and he takes the money."

"Doesn't tell me much that I can use, but thanks a lot, Sandy. Maybe I can ask Jennifer about a full name for Zack. She won't give it to me if she knows what I'm doing though. Have to handle it with a little finesse, I guess. I owe you one, Sandy. How about lunch at the Malden diner? Today, at twelve o'clock?"

"You don't owe me. But sure, I'd love to have lunch with you. It may be 12:05 though," Sandy laughed.

After Sandy and Ellen were seated, drinking tea while waiting on their lunch, Ron Brady approached their table.

"Well, well, I can't believe what I'm seeing. The two most beautiful ladies in the whole county."

Sandy beamed.

Ellen smiled, saying, "Those kind of compliments can get you into all kinds of trouble."

After a brief conversation, Ellen asked Ron to join them. She noticed how Sandy's countenance brightened when he accepted.

Ellen thanked Ron sincerely for the puppy he had given her. "How did you know I had always wanted a Rotty-Great Dane cross?"

"Well, I had inside info," he said. Then laughing, he restated his answer. "No...not really...it was just a fortuitous accident, I guess."

Ellen was sure he had gotten that information from someone who knew her well. It seemed too much of a coincidence. But who? Bud was the only one that would have known.

*Oh, yeah. Bud had surely mentioned Ellen's desire for that kind of a cross to Lila when they were married, and she must have passed the information on to Ron. So he had seen her recently then.*

Ellen had wanted that particular canine cross since

high school. Her best friend had one. It was the most loving, protective dog she had ever known.

Most of the conversation during lunch was just chitchat. Thinking she might get useful information, however, Ellen asked, "Have you seen Mr. Zachary lately? I think we finally have a Rogue-proof fence."

"Zachary? You mean Zack? His name is not Zachary. It's Isaac...Daniel Isaac Cunningham. Real nice guy. And yeah, the fence must be holding Old Rogue...or he's just behaving himself."

When Sandy finally took her eyes off of Ron, Ellen gave her a subtle nod and raised her eyebrows. Sandy seemed to have gotten the message. Ellen hoped she understood. Ellen wanted her to get on the net and check out Daniel Isaac Cunningham.

Ron had remembered Sandy from high school, and they asked about old acquaintances and retold old stories. The hour passed quickly and Ron had to leave. He asked Ellen if she would like to have dinner with him and see a movie on Friday night.

Ellen noticed the look on Sandy's face and said, "I'd love to, Ron, but I'm not sure I can make it. Can I let you know?"

"Sure. I'll call you in a couple of days. Okay?"

On her way home after the good-byes, Ellen thought about Sandy's reaction to Ron.

*She's really crazy about him. That's obvious. They would make a nice couple. But if he starts dating her, who will I ever get to go out with?*

Ellen had great affection for Ron. She knew, though, it would never be anything but a solid, enduring friendship. She couldn't *make* herself feel something that just wasn't there—even if he was a peach of a guy and as sweet as a sugarplum. Did she owe it to her good friend to back off and see if Ron would eventually feel about Sandy as she did about him? She would like them to be happy together…if it worked out that way. But the thought of being alone was depressing. Still it was downright wrong to stand in the way of a serious relationship just because she was lonely.

*Guess I'll just have to work harder, take up a new hobby or something. Or maybe I'll get on the net and find some guy who is as alone as I am…but never wants to marry.*

Somehow that thought was even more depressing.

As Ellen neared her home, she met a black vehicle equipped with spotlights on the sides and long antennas. *Looks like an unmarked police car,* she thought.

About a half mile further down the road, she met a red burgundy truck. Ellen was too concerned with negotiating the narrowed road where they met to notice if Jennifer accompanied Zack. Further on she met another black vehicle, equipped just like the first.

*Why would the sheriff or law enforcement be escorting Zack anywhere? Oh, Jeez! I have been playing detective so intently that I am now seeing cops and robbers everywhere,* she told herself.

Upon reaching her backyard, Brady made her welcome. She had chained him to the corner brace of her back patio. He was jumping up and down, straining at the end of his chain and whining for attention. After telling him "no" several times and praising him when he stopped for a minute, she dropped to her knees and rubbed down his coat. She released the chain from his collar, hugged him and told him what a good boy he was. He lapped it up. He wanted to rough house. She obliged.

*If he's going to be as loving and protective as I want him to be, he has to love me and know that we are inseparable buddies…and he has to know I love my cats too,* she reasoned.

Ellen went into the house and took the bag of washed and chilled greens from the refrigerator. She would take them to Jennifer before it got late enough to do her chores.

Jennifer was not at home, so Ellen went to Zack's house. "Guess this is home to her now," she murmured.

Jennifer came out on the front porch and thanked Ellen profusely. "Oh Bud loves lettuce and green onions with chopped radishes and an oil and vinegar dressing," she exclaimed.

*He sure did,* thought Ellen, *and you must too—you or Zack—since you seem so happy to get them.* She noticed Jennifer's choice of words, "Bud loves" as if he were present. Ellen liked to think of him that way too.

Jennifer asked Ellen to wait while she refrigerated the bag of goodies, but did not ask her in. "Don't leave. I'll be back in a sec," Jennifer said. "I want to show you Zack's yard. He needs some landscaping, and he wants you to do it."

When Jennifer returned, Ellen said, "I'm not a landscaper. And besides I'm too busy to take on a project like that right now."

She had mixed emotions about the offer. She would like to take on the job. His yard could be made into a lovely, peaceful haven of joy. But she didn't need the pressure of his presence, especially with his attachment to Jennifer always so obvious.

"No, I'm definitely not interested. Thank him kindly though."

She left before she could reconsider. Tears filled her eyes as she drove away. *What am I anyway? A fifth wheel? More like a third party on an intimate date.*

First, there was Sandy and Ron. Was she in their way? And then, there was Jennifer and Zack. She would not come between them, it was obvious. Was she what is called "the odd man out?"

Whatever it was called, it was a terribly unhappy feeling. She had no one to talk to. No one to hold her and she needed that more than anything right now.

*If only Bud were here,* she thought as she struggled to throw off the sorrow that overwhelmed her.

After Ellen got home, she tried to take a short nap, but could not fall asleep. Instead, she did some accounting and paid a few bills.

When she was ready to check her cows, she took Brady with her. He was eager to get into the truck and ride. Once on the ground, however, he was intimidated by the huge creatures that came towards him with their heads lowered, checking him out. He ran under the truck.

Finally he came out, but stayed close to Ellen's heels. After a bit, when the counting was done, Ellen stopped and patted his head telling him, "You'll work out fine. You're really a good boy."

He wagged his tail and licked her hand before jumping into the truck.

Ellen pulled back into her yard and let Brady out just as a copper colored Cadillac pulled into her drive. After parking close to Ellen's truck, the door opened and Lila stuck one long leg after the other out and stood tall on spike heels. She wore tight shorts; so short that Ellen could see the bottom curve of her buttocks when she walked.

"Gracious, Lila, with all that money your lover has, I would think you could afford to buy some clothes to cover your butt."

Ellen knew she had to be critical or Lila wouldn't think it normal. It wasn't difficult to do. She naturally disapproved of almost everything Lila did. And she had usually been pretty vocal about her opinions.

"I didn't get that restraining order you promised, so

I thought I must be welcome." Lila haughtily preened and rubbed her hands down over her hips.

"Very sensuous, Lila, but there are no guys here to impress."

Ellen took hold of Brady's collar and hooked it back to the chain on the patio corner post. She noticed Old Yowler and Miss Muffy at the edge of the yard, studying the situation.

She started towards her back door. "What do you want, Lila?"

"Just wanted to chat for a minute. Besides, I have a message for you."

*What could that be?* Ellen wondered. *I hope she has some information about Bud as well.*

Lila followed her into the house. Ellen washed her hands and went into the kitchen.

"I'm going to have a sandwich and glass of milk. Would you care for something?" she asked.

"Whoo...ee! Milk! No thanks. Don't you have anything decent to drink?"

"Depends on what you call decent. I have a varied assortment of what *you* probably call decent over there in the cabinet. If you want to mix your own."

Lila did. She went to the cupboard and opened the door. "Oh, boy! You have quite a stash here!" Lila was delighted.

Ellen ignored her. *Just let her get enough booze in her to start babbling,* she thought. *The less food she eats, the better, so I'll just skip dessert myself...so she won't eat any of that scrumptious cherry pie.*

About halfway through her sandwich, Lila said, "I talked to your ex again last night. Wants very much to talk to you and here is his number." She pushed a business card across the table. "Says, please call him."

"No thanks. If he wants to talk, he can call me.

Maybe I'll accept the call. Maybe not. Depends on my frame of mind."

Ellen took Harry's business card, tore it to shreds and tossed it into the wastebasket. She cleared away the dishes, poured herself a glass of tea and went into the den. Lila mixed herself another drink and followed.

"Sure is pretty out here in the country, but too quiet to suit me. I like lots of noise and things to do."

"There's lots to do here. Just not the kind of things you do," replied Ellen.

"Yeah, well Carlo and me, we like to go to the club. He wins a lot at the casino in Amber City too. I think it's a kick back from his buddy that runs it, you know. Carlo supplies him and he's real grateful."

"I like going to Bellows sometimes, myself," Ellen lied.

There were only two casinos in Amber City, and Ellen was fishing for which one Lila frequented.

"Oh, we don't ever go there. Johnny runs the one on Highway 77 just outta town. Carlo always wins there. I mean big time!"

"This Johnny surely doesn't kick back *too* much, just for a personal supply of smack or weed," Ellen taunted.

"Oh, no! Not a personal supply. He distributes to lots of dealers, so it's in the millions. He's no small town smuck."

"That kind of thing can get you into trouble, Lila. Aren't you worried about being close to all that illegal stuff?"

"Naw, Carlo can take care of me. He's got lots of firepower behind him." She giggled. "He can outgun ever' body—probably all at one time." She giggled again.

"He must have a cannon or a rocket powered missile or something then," Ellen retorted.

"AK 47s, shotguns and all sorts of illegals. He makes a lot off a them too," she said.

"By the way, have you heard any more about where Bud is?"

*She's finally getting down to the reason she's here,* thought Ellen.

"No. The sheriff can't figure it out."

"Typical dumb ass," Lila giggled. "Some people think he's with this secret agent man called Sid."

Ellen was all ears. "How do you know about this guy Sid? Who is he anyway? Why would he have Bud?"

"Protecting him, they think."

"From whom. Who would want to harm Bud?"

Ellen knew she had made a mistake. Lila's eyes focused on her. Part of the glaze disappeared.

"Don't know anything 'bout it. Just heard that somewhere." she said. She started to get another drink.

"Lila, if you're driving, maybe you better not drink any more. You might smash up your pretty car."

"Yeah, guess you're right. I gotta go anyhow. Carlo'll be back in an hour or so."

As she was leaving, Lila passed by the post where Brady was tethered. He moved out of her way.

"Don't let this mongrel get as mean as that other hound you had," she ordered. She got in her car and drove away.

*Look who's calling who a mongrel,* Ellen thought and she unhook Brady's collar from his chain and patted his head.

Ellen immediately called Jennifer at Zack's house. Jennifer answered the phone. *How cozy! Guess it really is her home now.*

"Jen, Lila just left here. I plied her with liquor—didn't take much. She said that she hears they—whoever that is—believe Bud is alive. That he's being protected by a secret agent man—as she put it—called Sid."

There was silence for a few seconds.

"Jen, are you there?"

"Yeah. I was just trying to figure who they might be and how they would know that."

"Jeez, I guess they must be the people who are after him, and they must have gotten the information through a leak in the department somewhere, as Sheriff Hewitt intimated. I just hope and pray this Sid guy is good at his job."

"Ell, you need to quit snooping. If you get too close and too much information, your life will be in even more danger."

"*More* danger? What do you mean, more?"

"Uh, well… if it's Lila and she and her buddies are after Bud and if they get him, then I'm next. After that, you're the only surviving relative, and you're next. But if you get info that proves they're guilty of murder or even attempted murder, you're on the top of the list…now."

"Well, Jen, I gotta know where Bud is or what happened to him. But I'll be careful," she promised.

Ellen brought Brady in, fed him and played with him for a bit, before putting him in his cage. Old Yowler and Miss Muffy were hesitant, but eventually hurried through the den into the kitchen when Ellen opened the door for them. After they finished their meal, Ellen got down on the floor and played with them where Brady could watch it all. He had to see that she loved her cats too.

All the work was done, so Brady was put in the utility room. The cats ran out quickly into the darkness. Ellen prepared for bed. She slipped into a negligee, wondering how Jennifer looked in a negligee with her rounded tummy. She fought back tears as she thought how cruel and unthinking Jennifer and Zack could be. He shouldn't seem to offer her his closeness and then back off. He shouldn't offer her a job either. She had no right to expect that he would respond to her, just because she had feelings for him. But the insensitive jerk must know how she felt about him. He didn't have to make it worse. Maybe most women reacted to him the same way, and he just saw it as something he had to ignore. He was evidently somewhat of a rogue himself. Still he should not tease her feelings as if they didn't matter.

*Guess he never loved anyone that didn't love him back. My feelings shouldn't change his and Jennifer's relationship, but I'll be damned if I'll stick around and watch their togetherness.* She felt her anger rise. *Or, maybe I'll just gut it up and take that job after all! I have to get over this stupid thing I have for him. I'm glad he has Jennifer. It helps me keep that promise I made to myself, that I almost forgot, to never ever get hooked up with another guy.*

# Chapter 11

Ellen hurried through her regular procedures the following morning as quickly as possible. When she counted her cows, she was one short.

*Oh, no, not this morning. I wanted to catch the sheriff and convey everything I learned from Lila.*

Because driving through the pastures in her truck could be hazardous, Ellen rarely did so. The grass and small brushy limbs in some places were hard on the undercarriage and in contact with a hot muffler could easily cause a fire. This morning she would only drive in some of the more cleared areas and walk when necessary.

*Guess I had better mow my pasture soon,* she thought.

It wasn't long before she spied Agnes, one of her pregnant cows, ensconced in a grove of black jack trees, chewing her cud.

"Ah, hah…getting ready to have that baby, are we?" Ellen spoke to her cow.

Agnes was a veteran at having babies. This would be her fifth calf. Ellen didn't expect Agnes to have any difficulty delivering. Experienced mother cows, if they were in good health and not overfed, usually didn't need help calving. But there was always a chance that an abnormal problem would arise.

Agnes was not far into her labor. The fact that she was still chewing her cud was also an indicator she was not yet in much pain. It would probably take all day.

Ellen would have plenty of time to talk to Sheriff Hewitt and even have coffee with any of the deputies still in the office. One of them was surely the "leak" who passed information on to Carlo Rodriquez.

118

Getting back to her house, she took time to rub down Brady and play with him a bit. The "how to" book cautioned not to miss one day of training. She went through the routine of playing with Old Yowler where Brady could watch her. Miss Muffy was hypnotized by a gopher mound in the yard. She did not come in for breakfast. Perhaps she viewed the gopher as her breakfast.

Ellen skipped her own breakfast in order to expedite the delivery of what could be significant news to the sheriff. She was anxious to know what Sheriff Hewitt would think of Lila's admissions.

The sheriff was just getting a cup of coffee when Ellen tapped on the door to his private office. He offered her a cup. She was glad to accept.

"You have made my day!" She thanked him.

"Before you ask, Ellen, I have some feelers out there. Unfortunately, I don't have concrete proof of what I need before divulging any secrets."

"Well, I have some news you may find interesting."

She proceeded to convey the information about Bud being protected by an agent called Sid.

She was disappointed when the sheriff only said, "H'mm."

*He already knew that*, she thought.

She continued with all the other things Lila had revealed to her. She told him about the kickbacks to Carlo from a Johnny who ran the "Elite Pickins" casino on Highway 77 and relayed Lila's comments about the weapons.

The sheriff seemed to grow more interested now. "Would you consent to a wiretap—a bug under your kitchen table—just to monitor what else Lila might want to tell you?"

"I would be absolutely delighted." Ellen agreed to help. "Is there anything special you want to know?"

"We need to know who delivers both the drugs and the weapons and where they come from and when they arrive. But if you ask those questions, she will know you are probing for information. Whatever you do, little lady, do not let her know you have the slightest interest in her associates. Just let her ramble. We'll take what we can get. These people are extremely dangerous. You can't become personally involved."

*Well, I guess I already am,* Ellen thought. *If I don't go after what I need, I may never get it. Now I know what takes you so long.* But she agreed to try and play it cool.

Sheriff Hewitt stared at Ellen intently for a few seconds. For an instant, he seemed on the verge of revealing something. Ultimately, however, he did not.

*What is it with these people? First Jennifer, then Ron, then Zack and now Sheriff Hewitt. What is it they want to tell me, but can't? Oh, God,* she pleaded with all her heart, *don't let it be bad news about Bud. If the news is bad...really bad, maybe that's why Jennifer apparently feels so free to be with Zack.*

"I'll send someone out to bug your table this afternoon," he chuckled. "Any specific time better for you?"

"Just call me before you come to make sure I'm not away from my house," she said. "And that Lila's not there," she added.

Two deputies were in the outer office as Ellen walked through. They offered her an apple fritter and a second cup'a "Joe."

"You guys are super great," she said. "How did you know I missed my breakfast?"

They introduced themselves as Cecil White, a younger, sweet-faced new member of the force, and John Kribbs, an older, blond, confident veteran.

"I had a classmate at Mason High named Sara Kribbs. We were both cheerleaders. Would she have been your sister, perhaps?" she asked Kribbs.

"Yes, I would think so. She was a cheerleader. Blond hair, blue eyes and about 5' 7". Smart kid. Always made the honor roll."

"Yep, that was Sara. Tell her 'hi' for me."

As they continued to chat, Ellen found out John was married, had three kids and was expecting a fourth. *Well, it's not him. He's not the leak. He's a solid citizen. On the other hand...maybe he needed some extra money...though I doubt it.*

Cecil White was pleasant, though he said very little. He was engrossed in paper work.

Ellen was beginning to understand why investigations took so long. There was just too much guess work and so hard to get real proof. For even though Lila had raised the insurance payout from $300,000 to $500,000, and had asked how soon she could collect without proof of death, all of which looked suspicious, she had done nothing illegal. There was no concrete evidence of any foul play against her, even though they had found her button at the bloody scene from which Bud had disappeared.

Ellen thanked them both for the coffee and fritter and hurried home to check on Agnes.

Miss Muffy was still sitting motionless, intently watching for something delectable to appear from out of the loose dirt around a hole in the ground. She took no notice as Ellen drove through the yard.

Ellen chuckled. *That dude doesn't have a chance. Miss Muffy will sit there all day, if necessary, waiting for a head to pop up out of that hole. She may be tired, but she'll still be quick enough to catch him.*

Miss Muffy was a persistent adversary who always won.

*Patience and persistence.* *Good qualities for felines and human beings alike,* thought Ellen.

Agnes had moved to a different clump of trees, but exhibited no progress in the birthing ordeal. Ellen would keep tabs on her throughout the day.

Since Ellen had enjoyed an apple fritter on the sheriff's tab, she would treat the guys, whom she expected that afternoon, to a peach cobbler and ice cream. So when they arrived, she had a fresh pot of coffee and cobbler ready to serve as soon as they finished with her table. They decided to bug the coffee table as well.

One deputy remarked, "Maybe Lila will want to set in here and rest if she gets really tanked."

*Sounds like he knows her well,* Ellen reflected. *Just how well? Would he tell her about the wire taps? I need to find out more about his past.*

Ron was not with the two that came to install the listening devices, but he did call later. "You'll have to be careful and not talk about your secrets and no hugging on the couch," he jokingly instructed her. "You are, in fact, on Candid Camera."

It *was* a little restrictive but not too uncomfortable. It was worth it if it would help find Bud.

Ellen checked on Agnes a couple more times during the afternoon. No progress was evident, and Agnes was getting restless. Ellen was beginning to get anxious herself.

Miss Muffy just sat and stared at that intriguing hole in the ground.

Before Ellen was ready to feed and count cows, she heard an agitated bawling at her barn gate. She ignored it for a short time, but went to check it out when it continued. Agnes had come to the barn. She was walking around in circles, occasionally stopping and looking towards the house. She bawled her discomfort. Ellen wasn't surprised. Whenever Agnes knew she needed help, she would do just that.

Once she had been bitten by a snake and was in terrible pain. And when she had a bad case of woody tongue, she let Ellen know before Ellen ever suspected she had a problem.

After hitching to her trailer and backing up to the loading ramp, Ellen opened the gate to the loading chute. Agnes knew what to do. She immediately went down the chute and into the trailer. It was a marvel. Ellen wished all her cows were that easy to load. She had called the vet and he agreed to stay overtime to take care of her cow. It would cost extra, but this precious bovine creature was worth it.

The calf was breach, butt first. It could never have been delivered without help. It had to be pushed forward until the vet could get the feet pulled back and out first. Then with an incision and forceps, the calf was born. Agnes gave a loud groan of relief. Sadly, the baby was dead, but no longer a threat to mama, who stood utterly still while the vet inserted two large pills and administered an injection of antibiotics. She was in a short chute, but not head caught.

"Amazing," the vet said. "She must be in shock."

The calf was a nice big one, which was the whole problem. It had probably been too big to turn the last time it should have, hence the breach birth. Agnes turned and sniffed her baby's body; she knew it was gone.

Ellen backed up to the loading ramp and Agnes got in the trailer without hesitation. The vet would dispose of the carcass. Ellen drove home.

Upon arrival at the barn, Ellen opened the trailer door. Mooing softly, the distressed mother stepped out on the ground. Looking all around, she then got back into the trailer, sniffing every inch of the floor. Stepping out again, she sniffed all around the trailer. Certain there was no baby there needing her attention, she left and went back to the herd. She had always been a good mama.

Miss Muffy was no longer sitting at the gopher mound.

*She caught him!* Ellen was positive.

Ellen entered the house, walked to the front door and discovered a gopher on the step, partially devoured. Miss Muffy had indeed viewed him as breakfast—well, supper, by the time she finally caught him.

Brady was ready for a romp. Ellen did him the favor. Together, they went for a walk down by Sediment Creek. All sorts of things caught his interest, especially a squirrel that ran up a tree and out of reach. He did a lot of complaining about that.

Back at her house, Ellen went through the regular routine for the cats and her lovable pooch. She was tired and went to bed a little earlier than usual.

When she passed by her table, she said, "Good night, guys" to the listening devices beneath it.

It was raining the next morning when Ellen walked past her table. Not knowing whether anyone was listening or not, she said, "Good morning, guys. Don't forget your umbrellas."

She had intended to work in her garden, since she had gotten somewhat behind. The rain had changed that. "Oh, well, I do love the rain. And at least I won't have to water now."

Ellen's bull yearlings were ready to sell, and she needed to put an ad in the *Malden Daily News*. She needed groceries as well, so she decided to drive into town. After finishing her regular tasks and eating breakfast, she prepared the ad for the paper, hoping it would get quick results.

*No point in hanging onto livestock after they reached their prime. It would only cost money.*

Ellen called Sandy and asked her if she would like to have lunch at the Malden Diner.

"Sure would," Sandy replied, "and I have some info about Zack for you."

"I'll just get it at lunchtime, okay?"

"Well...okay."

"See you at 12:05."

Sandy laughed, "Sure thing, see ya there."

Ellen didn't want anyone in the sheriff's office to know she was checking up on Zack. So she couldn't have a conversation about him above her table. She wondered if Ron had picked up on her luncheon date with Sandy. He usually ate at the diner anyway.

After Ellen and Sandy were seated and drinking their customary glass of tea, Sandy pulled some papers from her purse.

"Here's what I found out about Zack."

Ellen saw Ron enter the diner.

"Is everything you learned written down here? Is there anything else to add?" she asked as she put the papers in her purse. "Here comes Ron and I don't want your favorite deputy to know I'm checking up on Zack. Okay?"

"Okay," was Sandy's breathless reply.

Ron stopped to chat a moment with other deputies at a table nearby, then approached Ellen and Sandy.

"Can I invite myself to enjoy your company or is it strictly girl talk today?"

Ellen bid him welcome, "Even if it were, we'd change it just for you."

Sandy's smile revealed her pleasure at his presence. Their conversation was somewhat more animated than it had been during their previous luncheon. Ellen sort of sat back and watched Sandy blossom. Ron seemed to enjoy the hour a lot. Still, when it was time to leave, he asked Ellen if she were free Friday night.

Sandy's smile disappeared and she stiffened.

Ellen said, "Well, uh...mm...Sandy and I sort of decided we'd have popcorn and watch a movie at my house on Friday night. Can you still make it, Sandy?"

Sandy hid well her surprise at Ellen's statement. "Yes, I can, but don't let me keep you from going *out* to a movie."

"Tell you what. Why don't we all have dinner at my house? Six thirty, Friday night. And Ron, bring a friend or two, we may play canasta or poker or something instead. We'll have steaks and then watch a movie or something. Okay?"

"Steaks for a crowd? Steaks are pretty expensive. Are you sure?"

"Yeah, I grow my own steaks, you know. Just tell me how many to expect."

Sandy's eyes sparkled with anticipation. Ellen had mixed emotions. She thought Sandy and Ron would be good together, but she hoped she didn't lose a dear friend in the process. Maybe Ron would still call to chat once in a while...and she knew Sandy would.

Driving home, Ellen remembered what was under her table.

*Oh shoot. I wonder if they can turn off the bug temporarily. Maybe we'll eat outside. Have a cookout. That would settle it. It will let the guys help with the cooking too,* she decided.

She was almost home when the rain stopped except for a slight sprinkling. As Ellen approached Bud's house she saw papers on the ground around his mailbox.

*Good gosh! Did the postman just throw the mail at*

126

*the box in the rain?*

She stopped, picking up the letters and papers to put them back in the box, when she noticed one in particular. It was bulky and so damp the envelope had come open. The return address was "Globe Life Insurance."

Who had a better right to read Bud's mail, now that he was missing? Ellen stuffed down any feelings of guilt and unfolded the document. It was a policy on Bud with a new beneficiary, one Jennifer Phillips.

How? Who? It was certainly something that should have been done, but who had done it? Obviously, Jennifer and Zack. She checked the signature. Someone had done an excellent job of forgery. Perhaps with the help of a computer. It was Bud's signature exactly.

Ellen was eager to read all the information Sandy had given her about Zack. So as soon as she was home, she sat at the table and pulled the papers from her purse.

He was born in Ateeka County and was only two years older than Ellen. He had one brother, Matt, and one sister, Patricia. His parents still resided in Ateeka County.

He had graduated from Oklahoma University with a degree in criminology and law enforcement and had worked for the Norman Police Department for several years. He had achieved the rank of captain and had several commendations. Then nothing. All was blank. There was no record of where he was or what he was doing. It didn't even show he was living next door to Ellen.

Sandy had underlined in black marker his initials <u>D</u>aniel <u>I</u>saac <u>C</u>unningham.

*Why did she do that? DIC! Is that supposed to mean something? Maybe he was a dick—like Dick Tracy, a detective.* Ellen would have to ask Sandy what she meant.

She stored the papers in her desk, underneath some seed catalogs.

Before Ellen retired that evening, she noticed a message on her phone. Zack wanted to talk to her about doing his yard.

*Do I have enough self-control to do that?* she worried. *I love that man! I want that man...so much I cannot possibly hide it. What in the name of heaven am I supposed to do?*

She could not speak to him now. She would make that decision in the morning.

# Chapter 12

The next morning, Ellen felt rested and more confident. She would have to accept things the way they were with Zack and Jennifer. She would have to control her emotions, to put her own feelings out of her mind and eventually out of her heart. She couldn't hide from them forever.

Yes, she would do Zack's yard.

After her livestock were fed and counted, Ellen spent extra time with Brady, Old Yowler and Miss Muffy. She was pleased with their progress in accepting each other. Soon she could put them together without restraint to see just how effective her efforts had been.

Brady was a sweet dog. He obeyed her almost always without hesitation and seemed to be concerned about her safety.

Ellen was having trouble with her electric range. She decided she had better call a repairman and have it checked out. When the electrician arrived, her pooch, usually a friendly dog, growled and followed him to the door. When Ellen admitted the rather scruffy looking fellow and started to close the door, the pup put his weight against it with force.

"Okay. If you must, come on in," Ellen said.

Brady placed himself between Ellen and the man constantly. He watched the guy as though he thought he might steal his bone. Ellen thought her dog made the repairman very nervous. The man dropped a rather large wrench, which caused her Rottweiler to growl and lunge toward him, the scruff of his neck standing on end. Ellen grabbed his collar and pulled him back, talking to him constantly, trying to calm him down. But Ellen never put him outside. She trusted his instincts. If

Brady thought the man needed watching, Ellen would let Brady watch him. When the man left, her protector, seemingly satisfied, went back outside to pursue his doggy interests.

Ellen watched him through the window. He ran and jumped, with all four feet high in the air, pursuing grasshoppers, she supposed. He caught a lot of them and seemed to enjoy doing it, as well as the tasty morsels they must have been. As he cornered the house, Ellen smiled at his exuberance. He moved like a "hopper" himself.

Going into the den, Ellen noticed a roadrunner, sprinting alongside her driveway.

During the last few weeks, she had often seen a pair of them. They were staying much closer to her house than usual.

*They have learned, like the rabbits have, that coyotes don't venture close to the human den,* Ellen guessed.

As she watched the chaparral, another one of the snake-eating birds appeared. This one was much smaller, a baby roadrunner, the first Ellen had ever seen. It was not newly hatched, though. It had all its feathers, even the long ones in the tail that made him look so awkward. It appeared his mother was trying to teach him to avoid predators. She ran from clumps of grass to brushy stumps, to clusters of weeds, anything that would afford cover for her. Baby bird stayed behind her, perhaps thirty feet or so. He took shelter in clumps that she had just left. He waited until she left the next safe haven before he left his and ran to the one she had vacated. Ellen was fascinated. These birds were worth their weight in gold.

After approximately ten to fifteen minutes, the baby bird left his safety cover and ran just a few feet. He stopped and watched mother bird for a bit, then turned and went back into the last shelter.

"You should have read my 'how to train book,' mother bird. You have overworked your student." Ellen laughed. What a wonderful thing to have witnessed. She hoped the roadrunners were able to proliferate safely. Moments like these were what made life worth living.

She turned from the window. She had procrastinated long enough. She had to call her mighty-fine-neighbor who drove a burgundy truck.

"*Comment allez vous*," she greeted him

"Ellie?" he questioned.

"*Oui, bonjour, monsieur.*"

"Oh, come on now, you know I don't speak French."

She laughed. Anything to break the tension and start the conversation.

"Good morning, Zack. How be you?"

"You must be in good spirits this morning."

"Not really. Trying to get there though," she replied.

"Have you decided to landscape my yard?"

"Well, I guess I can do some work on that, but keep in mind I'm not a landscaper."

"I'm sure you'll do," he said. "Would you like to come over and give me some ideas?"

"Not really. You're supposed to have the ideas. It's your yard. I just implement, or add to or beautify," she chuckled.

"What I want is for you to take charge and make it something you yourself would be proud of. I won't say money's not an object, but we may as well do it right to start with."

"Are you saying you have time right now?" she asked.

"Yes, as soon as it fits your schedule."

"I'll be there in about twenty minutes. Need to leash my dog."

When she arrived, Zack came out to greet her with coffee in hand. He offered to get her a cup.

"No thanks. Don't drink on the job."

He smiled at her attempted humor. "Okay, where do we start?"

She turned and looked at him. His blue eyes and broad shoulders interfered with her concentration.

"You really mean for me to just do what I want to?" she asked.

*Whoa! Don't think about that. Dangerous territory.* She cautioned herself.

"Yes, I do." He sounded absolutely sure. "What do I know about plants or trees and stuff?"

"No, you really have to give me some help here. What do you like? Roses, azaleas, peonies, sunflowers, cockleburs, poison ivy or what?" she teased.

"Don't need any cockleburs or poison ivy," he laughed.

His eyes twinkled. He had a dimple on his left check. He had one curl that wanted a life of its own.

*Keep your mind on your business, Ellen,* she commanded herself.

"Do you like lots of bright color or do you prefer mostly green, restful plants and trees?"

"I'd like a little of both, I think. Just a splash of color here and there maybe."

"Do you want to do just the front yard or the backyard too?" she asked.

"Let's just do the front for now. Maybe you will…"

He stopped. Moving his gaze over the softness of her throat and lingering on her mouth, his eyes finally raised to meet hers. His expression there caused her breath to catch sharply. A tightening sensation raced through her belly, and her heart sent a pounding pulse to her temples. She felt light-headed and looked away to clear her mind.

His voice was husky as he spoke. "Let's just do the front for now," he repeated.

Trying to keep it light and her mind on her business, Ellen quipped, "Ah, ha, need to check out my work first, huh? Okay. That's good business. I brought a camera and will take pictures. I can put those on my computer and fill in with various plants and shrubs to see what you prefer. It will take a few days to get those back to you."

"Excellent idea," he said. "I'm looking forward to seeing them." He was standing too close and getting that look in his eyes again. Softly, he continued, "And I have every confidence in you and your work."

She wanted his arms around her so desperately; she almost reached for him. Forcing herself to remember he was elsewhere committed, she quickly turned away, saying, "Thanks."

After taking pictures of every corner and section of Zack's yard from different angles, Ellen went home to experiment with different plants in different places, on paper of course.

She would do several different arrangements for each picture she had taken of Zack's yard. She would select what she thought were the best two or three of each and set them aside with a price quote on each to present to Zack.

She especially liked an ornamental grass corner that would make a striking year-around accent for his yard. It had one large white pampas grass plant in the precise corner. Shorter flame grass would be planted in a curve all around the front of the pampas grass.

Flame grass would start out green, but turn to a reddish-purple in the summer and finally exhibit white, silky flower heads and make a splendid backdrop all through winter.

Next, she would plant blue oat grass in a curve in front of the flame grass. The foliage on blue oat grass was really a blue-gray, but stays beautiful all winter. The whole arrangement would make a spectacular corner in Zack's yard. And it was perennial. No need to worry. It would be there next year if it received just a little TLC. Ellen hoped Zack would pick this arrangement. It had color, but was not too flamboyant.

It would take some time and effort, but she looked forward to the end results.

For the moment, however, she had other fish to fry.

Ellen had received several calls about the yearling bulls she had advertised for sale. One gentleman was particularly interested and said he might buy them all. He had a large spread in Texas and wanted quality "papas."

"A good bull can upgrade a herd of cattle pretty quick," he commented.

"Right," Ellen agreed. "Take a rangy old cow and cross her with a chunky, pure bred Limousin bull, and you'll get a really nice calf that's fifty percent Limousin to boot. That's a goodly increase in quality and price of your cattle in only one year."

Mr. Carlton, the Texas rancher, said, "I'll be there right about 2:00 o'clock. That be okay?"

"That'll work," Ellen answered.

"I'm bringin' my trailer so as I can bring 'em home with me if we can agree. See ya about 2 pm," he said and hung up the phone.

Indeed, he did arrive at precisely 2:00. As Ellen hoped, he liked her Limousins and bought them all. As he prepared to load them, he had a question to ask of her. Leaving his rig parked in the pasture not yet lined up with the loading chute and with the trailer gate open, he went to knock on Ellen's door.

"Ma'am, I forgot to bring my prod. Would you have one I could borrow?" he asked.

"No. Sorry. I never use a prod. I will help you load them though. I should have offered already," she apologized.

Ellen usually loaded all her cattle by herself...with a bucket of feed. She had not thought about him needing assistance.

When they reached the loading pens, Ellen laughed out loud. Agnes had loaded herself up. She was in Mr. Carlton's trailer.

*She must think good things happen when you go for a ride in a trailer. That or she thinks this trailer is going back to where she left her baby,* Ellen thought.

Ellen told Mr. Carlton the story about Agnes. He seemed to enjoy the tale. He told Ellen when he needed more bulls, he would call her.

She thanked him as she gave him her business card. "It says Wade Nursery, but as you see, I have cattle as well."

Ellen hoped as she watched him drive away that she would be doing more business with Mr. Carlton.

It was finally Friday, and Ellen had to prepare for the cookout. Some extra house cleaning was done. Steaks were taken out of the freezer. Potatoes were scrubbed and ready to wrap. The salad was ready, as was the tea, and the rolls were ready for the oven. There were several bottles of wine to choose from, if the ladies preferred, and a cherry pie for dessert, a la mode or not. And lots of beer. She had rented several movies, just in case.

All Ellen's chores were done, and Brady had enjoyed his romp with her. Ellen was sitting for a short rest when the phone rang. It was Lila.

"Thought I'd come out in a minute and see how you're doin'." She said.

"I can tell you over the phone in a few short sentences," Ellen responded. "Extremely tired and cranky."

"Well, I'll be out that way, anyway. I'll just drop by for a minute."

"Sorry, Lila, I'm busy tonight. I have company coming for dinner, and I can't set another plate. The table is full. What's so important anyway?"

"Nothing, just wanted to see if you had heard anything else about Bud. Who's going to be there tonight anyway?"

"No. I've heard nothing else about Bud. And it's just a few of us girls going to watch a home video. You'd be bored to death. Tomorrow would be better. Why don't you come then if you really need to come by."

Lila laughed. "Well, well...an invitation from Ellen, believe it or not! Thanks a lot. I'll see ya." She hung up.

Ellen wished she never had to see her again. Ever.

*Some things, no matter how unpleasant, just can't be avoided, like shoveling out the barn stall,* she thought.

Soon Sandy arrived, especially lovely in a pale pink pullover with snug fitting jeans. She brought some lemonade and a chocolate pie.

Bill and Maggie Stephens, whom Ellen knew slightly, came with Ron. He said another deputy, Wade Rogers, would be coming as well.

The guys had started the grill and were having a beer when a red burgundy truck pulled into the drive. When Zack opened his door and got out, a bouncing bundle of "happy" jumped out and ran sniffing around the patio. Brady had somehow gone to Zack's house.

---

Ellen hadn't put him on his leash. She usually didn't if she were at home. Why had the little goober gone to Zack's? She attached the chain to his collar and gave him a treat. No scolding followed. He wouldn't understand at this point why she was doing it.

Ellen felt obligated to ask Zack to stay, though she hoped he wouldn't. His presence kept her up tight.

"No, thanks. I won't crash your party." He glanced at Ron.

"No crash," Ellen assured him. "Have a beer at least."

He accepted.

Steaks were put on the grill, nice large ones. One for each of the six expected and a few extra, just in case.

The phone rang. It was Wade Rogers. He couldn't make it; some special incident at the bowling alley had resulted in extra duty for him.

"What are we going to do with these extra steaks?' someone asked. "Zack needs to stay."

"They really do smell great. Very tempting." Zack seemed to acquiesce.

"Stay, by all means," Ellen forced herself to say.

So he stayed and had another beer.

When everything was prepared and everyone was enjoying dinner, a copper Cadillac came down the drive and stopped close to the patio. Lila got out in tight-fitting pants, high heels and a revealing blouse. Ellen wanted to order her to leave, but controlled her anger. She wished she had locked the front gate.

"Why are you burning candles in the daylight?" Lila snickered.

"They are citronella. They keep away insects and unwanted pests," Ellen answered. She looked at Lila and added, "Well, most of them anyway. Thought you weren't coming until tomorrow night."

"Oh, I was just in the neighborhood." The look on her face said Lila was feeling one-upmanship.

*Guess because I hadn't wanted her to come and she came anyway and found a whole group of good-looking guys to charm, she thinks she's bested me on my own turf,* Ellen guessed.

"Thought you were only having the *girls* over tonight." Lila sneered.

"Well, their guys got free so they came along too," Ellen said without hesitation.

"Mind if I have a beer?" Lila asked.

"Help yourself. There's some hard stuff in the house if you care for it."

Lila did. She went into the house to mix herself a drink.

*Maybe she'll reveal even more with all this masculinity around,* Ellen hoped.

Ellen felt compelled to offer her a place at the table. Lila refused the food, but pulled up a chair. After some chatting and drinking, Lila began to grow friendly.

"Ron, sweetie, why haven't you called me? I've been neglected lately."

Ellen looked at Sandy. Sandy glanced first at Ron and then at Lila. Then clenched her jaw. Ron was clearly embarrassed.

"Heard you were pretty much with a steady partner," he said.

"Yeah, but I like an extra night occasionally…when Carlo's out of town, you know."

Ron glanced at Zack. Ellen thought she saw a slight dip of his head. Had Zack nodded "yes"?

"Well…okay, when will he be gone?" Ron asked.

Ellen knew what Ron was about.

Lila was delighted. She had crashed the party and made a date with Ellen's beau right in front of Ellen's guests!

"Next Friday night, as a matter of fact. He'll be gone all night. Has to go to Laredo. Just call me after 5 pm. He'll be gone by then."

*What a brazen hussy!*

Ellen wasn't really surprised, but this was a new low, even for Lila. Sandy looked at Ellen. Ellen could feel her anger. She pursed her lips and shook her head "no" to let Sandy know that would never happen. Ron said nothing, but looked at Zack.

Zack took charge. "Sure is a nice looking automobile you're driving. That yours? Or does he just let you drive it when he's not going to Laredo?"

Lila was indignant. "No! He don't drive my car, ever. He drives his own SUV, but he'll have an escort this time. A convoy really." She giggled.

Ellen thought the Sheriff's office had some valuable information now. Carlo was going on a drug run, and they knew the time and place. What a stroke of luck or was it genius? Ellen wondered at Zack's involvement.

None of them pursued it further. To do so might arouse Lila's suspicion and ruin it all.

Small talk continued until everyone had finished their dinner. Zack had to leave and graciously thanked Ellen for her invitation.

She said she was glad he had come and meant it. On several occasions during dinner, she had been aware that he was watching her. What did it mean? Anything? It put her somewhat on edge, but she liked it. Maybe too much.

As Zack started to leave, Lila tried to get his attention. "Why don't you stay for just one more drink? I really haven't got to talk to you at all. Everyone keeps interrupting."

Zack laughed. "*You'd* best not have another drink. Especially if you're driving home."

"Well, you could drive me home, couldn't you?"

Ellen wanted to slap her down, but looked away as Zack glanced at her.

Before he could answer, Lila added, "Maybe not…Carlo will be there."

Zack left. Lila went to sleep on the couch, and everyone else watched Bonnie Bedelia and Harrison Ford in "Presumed Innocent."

Ellen thought she understood why some people would kill for love.

Everyone seemed to have enjoyed the evening in spite of Lila who woke with a headache and went home in a huff. Ellen thought it fun, but was glad it was over. She was tired and needed some rest.

Her last thought before she fell asleep was *I'm doing a very poor job of putting my feelings out of my mind…let alone my heart.*

# Chapter 13

Leftovers and trimmings from all the steaks were saved from the night before, so Brady, Old Yowler and Miss Muffy had a great breakfast.

Ellen's garden was laden with vegetables ripening for the market. She had picked tomatoes, cantaloupes, squash and more green beans. From her greenhouse, she had selected several hanging baskets of weeping petunias, some begonias and ivy and even some beautiful sweet potato vines.

Ellen began to call her vendors and sold everything within the hour. The buyers were familiar with Ellen's plants and produce, as well as her prices, and were always eager to purchase. Today was the first of many days that she would be picking and delivering, usually every other day for at least six weeks.

Now the deliveries would have to be made. Brady wanted to go along, and for a minute she considered taking him. No, it would be too much of a hassle. She leashed him in the shade and loaded her flowers into the cab of her truck. They were the most fragile and needed protection from the wind. With only a slight breeze, driving created its own wind, and tender plants needed to be covered.

Ellen had a camper for her vehicle, but didn't like to mess with it if she could avoid it. The camper afforded good cover for Ellen's flower and delicate plants, but it was time consuming to put on and take off. If transporting only produce such as potatoes, melons, tomatoes and the like, which could handle the breeze, she preferred not to take the time to put on the camper. She would, however, deliver as quickly as possible to keep her freshly picked garden bounty from the sun.

As soon as Ellen finished all her deliveries, she returned to unleash Brady. She noticed Old Yowler and Miss Muffy asleep in the shade of the same tree where he was chained. Hallelujah! They trusted each other.

She unleashed Brady, who paid the cats no mind. He went to catch grasshoppers, jumping high in the air and bounding around.

*If he were going to catch grasshoppers and they jumped, he had to jump too, didn't he?* She laughed. *What a comical sight.*

Ellen knew she had to get busy on the project for Zack's yard. She hoped she could be more in charge of her emotions. It seemed she was always on the verge of tears lately, unusual for her.

Even though it was lunchtime, she wasn't hungry. She decided to have coffee and a couple of cookies she had purchased from the high school band. She chose one happy face cookie with chocolate chip eyes and nose. The other was heart-shaped and covered with strawberry icing. She placed them on the table while she poured and sweetened her coffee.

Brady was scratching at the door. She let him in and filled his water bowl before returning to the dining area. There she found Brady finishing off the crumbs of her strawberry iced heart, her favorite.

"Dadgummit, you renegade! You would annihilate my *heart*!"

Thinking what she had said was perfectly applicable to what Zack had done, she let the unhappiness she felt settle onto her immediate source of irritation, her astonished pup.

"Get out. Just go!" She opened the door, ordering him to leave." Chastised, her furry protector was slinking away, his tail between his legs. Ellen was filled with remorse and emptiness as she watched him go. Tears stung her eyes and she softly modified her command.

"But don't go far."

He got the message. His head lifted. Wagging his tail, he came back to the door. She joined him on the step, hugging him and apologizing. Her eyes brimming with heartfelt tears, she gave way to a tumult of emotions she could no longer hide...but Brady would never tell.

Later she managed to concentrate on putting together a plan for Zack's approval. First she had to decide on what to plant in his yard.

Crepe myrtle grew amazingly well in Oklahoma and bloomed all summer. It took little effort to maintain except for the initial trim. Most homeowners in the area seemed to prefer theirs trimmed into trees. Four of them, spaced along the eastern edge of Zack's yard, would be beautiful. She preferred the bright pink blossoms, but would check out Zack's color preference.

For the shady spots under his large trees, Ellen chose an assortment of Regal Blue hostas, red trinity, astilbe and lily of the valley. Taller plants would be planted closest around the tree and the smaller ones graduating from the edge. She would even stick in a couple of cinnamon ferns as well. A couple of special althea bushes in isolated spots would also be nice, ones that bloomed all summer and required almost no maintenance.

There had to be something to smell as well as to see. Roses. Maybe Fragrant Cloud. It would be beautiful all summer. It was a bright coral red and had a powerful fragrance of tangerine and oranges. She'd have to ask Zack if he liked the smell of oranges. And honeysuckle! It was wonderfully scented. Some planted close to where he parked his truck might be appreciated—just a joyous whiff of welcome each time he came home.

There were so many wonderful plants to choose

from, but she didn't want to go overboard at first. He could decide to add more later if he wished.

Ellen had purchased a package of assorted pictures. It contained all the flowers, shrubs and trees that grew in Oklahoma. She uploaded them to her computer, changing the size and layering them on her photos of Zack's house and yard. Then she started to work, piecing the scenes together.

Some of the flowers and shrubs Ellen could furnish from her own stock. For those she did not have in stock, she consulted her wholesale catalogs for recent prices.

As soon as she finished the plan, she realized it had not taken as long as she had thought it would. And the price would not be staggering. She hoped Zack would be pleased. Now the physical work would begin. First there was time for a stroll. Ellen and Brady took a romp down by Sediment Creek. It was cool under the shade of the pecan trees. The water was flowing and surprisingly cold compared to the air temperature. Spring fed creeks usually were.

Her exuberant pooch had a blast. Frogs in particular intrigued him. He would jump into the water as they leaped in, splashing Ellen if she were close by. She realized as she watched him that she must have him neutered soon. She didn't want to, but it was for his own protection. Neutered, he would have no interest in the female coyotes. She would not let them destroy her cherished pup.

Ellen loved her farm. She had been delighted that Bud wanted to be her partner in the work she loved. But with Bud now missing and gone so long and with Jennifer obviously attached to Zack, she was beginning to wonder if it might be best to sell out and move on.

She could take Brady, Old Yowler and Miss Muffy wherever she went, but what about all her cows? It would cost more to move them than to sell and repurchase, she imagined. And if she sold, who would ever understand her sweet Agnes? And to move all her equipment—it seemed staggering. But how could she stay? It seemed impossible. Maybe someone else would come along that would tweak her interest—maybe soon. Zack wasn't the only man in the universe and maybe—just maybe—she could love a different guy who could love her back. But she didn't really want that to happen. Good Gracious! All she really had to do was to tamp down this feeling she had for Zack.

She desperately needed someone to talk to. Where was Bud? They had to find him. But she didn't know of anything else she could do. Now she understood what Sheriff Hewitt meant. If all leads had been exhausted and there were no more bushes to shake, you were pretty much at a standstill until something else happened, or you had a new flash of insight. She prayed for both. She had reached the end of her rope.

*Just tie a knot and hang on! And pray a lot.*

Tears clouded her vision and trickled down her cheeks. Would she ever know happiness again? Would Bud ever be found? Would he ever be able to continue his life as planned, even if he were okay? Would he have to tamp down his emotions as well? Would their world right itself again? Would there be peace and harmony again someday? It didn't seem likely.

Work. That was the answer.

*Don't forget what it cost you so much to learn,* she cautioned herself.

It was true. Work! She would keep herself so busy she didn't have time to grieve or worry—no, that was not quite true. She would still worry and grieve, but somehow it would be subdued—pushed back to the outer edges of her conscious mind. And when she went to bed, she would be so tired she would sleep soundly through the night.

She would work harder. She would call Zack and get his approval of a plan and start digging holes and planting things. With that in mind, when she and Brady returned to the house, she called her mighty fine neighbor.

Hoping he wouldn't answer, she counted the rings. She wasn't ready to talk just yet.

"Hello,"

Her pulse rate quickened. The timbre of his voice was always so confident. She wondered if he had ever felt "odd man out"?

"Hello, I have some plans and pictures to show you when you have time." *Just another client,* she soothed her racing heart.

"Really? That was pretty fast. I'm anxious to see them, but I'm not sure when I can come by. Maybe tomorrow late or the next day."

Feeling a little rejected, after all the work she had done, Ellen wanted to say, *Just forget it. I'll mail them and you can stuff...or do whatever you want to with whatever you choose. Whoa ,girl! Just hang on for a few minutes; be reasonable 'til you get off the phone.*

Instead, she said, "Fine. Just let me know when it will fit into your schedule." *How wonderfully detached I sound,* she thought.

"Well, I'm not sure what time that will be, so why don't I just drop by your place on my way home? Tomorrow if I can possibly make it—if not, then I'll call. Okay?"

*I have schedules too, you jerk. I might even have a date. Did that ever occur to you?*

She toyed with the idea of verbally accosting him. Instead, she said, "That'll work," and hung up.

*It will work. It has to work. I'll make it work.* She tried to convince herself.

The next day Ellen busied herself with all the menial tasks that seemed to have gotten put aside while she had special things that consumed her attention. Things like trying to get information out of the sheriff's department—or Lila; things like building a fence that she hadn't expected to need.

She was intrigued with the idea of Carlo and his thugs getting caught on Friday night. That probably wouldn't tell her anything about Bud's whereabouts, but just maybe one of them would say something that would help locate her brother.

She knew Ron would be involved, and she was concerned about his safety. Maybe there would be SWAT teams and lots of other officers so that Ron's exposure would be minimal.

The next afternoon as Ellen was having a glass of tea, she looked out of her patio window. Brady was stretched out, asleep under the locust tree. Miss Muffy was curled up beside him with her head resting on his paw.

*Hallelujah! What a blessing! Some things do turn out right after all.*

She heard a motor and looked to see Ron coming down her drive. He got out of his car carrying a nice-sized watermelon and knocked on her door.

"What in the world! Did you get off duty early? And why did you buy a melon? I will have multitudes of them."

"Yeah, but this one is ripe now." He grinned. His eyes crinkled.

The melon was cold and exceptionally sweet. They enjoyed it and each other's company until Zack's name came up.

Ron was watching her closely and asked unexpectedly, "You love him, don't you?"

Ellen was astonished. She stared at Ron, not

knowing what to say. To deny it was folly. Ron had a right to know if he were in any way getting seriously interested in her, didn't he? She felt a glistening in her eyes.

"I thought so," Ron said softly.

"It's not that obvious, is it? It's all so preposterous! I try to push it aside, but it won't go."

She attempted to smile. "It really doesn't matter. Zack has blinders on where I am concerned, and he is already committed."

"Don't be too sure," he said.

He stood and pulled her out of her chair. He put his arms around her, saying, "It's okay, sweetheart. We really don't have a choice about such things, I guess."

She smiled at him and said. "I love you, Ron. You are terrific, and we will always be the best of buddies."

"That's a gift I gratefully accept," he said and hugged her again.

She stood on tiptoes and put her arms around him. She kissed him smack on the mouth.

Someone cleared his throat at the screen door and said, "Excuse me...am I interrupting?"

They turned to see Zack standing there, twirling his key ring on his finger.

"Well, what the hell do you think, buddy?" Ron laughed.

Zack evidently didn't think it was funny. He didn't laugh.

Ellen said, "Come in. You're earlier than I expected."

"I can come back later if this is a bad time," Zack offered.

"Don't be absurd," Ron said. "We just had a melon and now I have to run. Have a good planning session. See you, Ell." And he was gone.

Ellen was hurriedly clearing the table and felt uncomfortable.

"He's really a super guy," she commented.

"Well, I guess. He's really not my type," he replied rather brusquely.

Ellen quickly got the pictures and prices to show Zack. All of the things she had tediously put together for his yard seemed somehow irrelevant at the moment.

He watched her intently, refusing politely the tea or coffee she offered. Clearly he wanted to get down to business.

After looking at all the plans and pictures, he said, "These are all very good. Makes it hard to choose." His final choices were mostly Ellen's own favorites. "All of these for such a reasonable price?" he asked.

"Well, I had quite a lot of it in stock so there was no extra shipping, and it is rather late in the season so I was able to get some good prices."

When Zack offered part payment up-front, Ellen said. "If you wish, you can pay for the things I have to order. I have a good deal of the plants, trees and shrubs in stock. I can be starting with those, while we wait for the orders to arrive."

"Sounds great." He was still watching her closely. It made her feel awkward.

"So is it okay if I get started right away?"

"Yes, of course. Whenever you like. I'll be out of pocket for a couple of days, Friday and Saturday... until late, perhaps. But do whatever you think will work."

He stood to leave. Ellen put away her papers and reached for the check he had left on the desk.

His hand closed over her own.

*What! Had he changed his mind?*

She looked up. His eyes caught hers and held. She found it impossible to look away.

"Ellie," he whispered.

He moved closer. She couldn't breathe. He grabbed

her in his arms with a look of purpose. He kissed her hungrily, and just as eagerly she kissed him back. Against her wishes, she felt herself respond. He pulled her close and buried his face in her hair. She trembled. She felt she was losing her balance.

"Ellie, there are some things we need to discuss and it's too soon, but please hang on a little longer," he pleaded. "It won't be long now." He kissed her again, tenderly this time. She felt the tears well in her eyes and in spite of her rising desire, she said, "You're as bad as Old Rogue! What is it you want? A harem?"

"No."

But by the time he spoke, she was gone. Ellen left the room and was out the door, calling back, "I think you'd best leave now!"

He stared after her, a half-smile on his lips. He had the look of a man who was just assured of something he had hoped for.

Ellen decided that if Zack would be gone for a few days, she would get as much done on his yard as possible. So early the next morning, she began beautifying the landscape of her mighty fine neighbor.

She took her gardening tools and a few plants at a time and worked with dedication to accomplish her goals: to do a good landscape of Zack's yard and to push her feelings into oblivion.

She measured and removed grass where necessary, dug holes and used compost before setting in the chosen nursery items. Then came the edging and wood chips. The yard began to take shape.

Friday came and went. Ellen was uptight all day wanting to know what was going to happen with Carlo and his bad guys and exactly where it would all take place. She hoped fate would smile on the guys with the white hats, not the guys in the black SUV. By Saturday afternoon, Ellen could stand the suspense no longer. She called Ron at home.

"Sorry to bother you, but I had to know how you are."

"I'm okay. It was just a lot of time and tension and no sleep, so I was catching up."

"What happened with Carlo and his henchmen? Did you get that vermin behind bars?

"Well, yes and no. We got the guys in two cars and lots of guns and drugs. Don't know how much just yet. But Carlo and another carload got away. We have five of his guys behind bars, though."

"Was anyone hurt?"

"No, we pretty much got the drop on them, except Carlo and one other car that was hanging back. They took off like a rocket when we reached the point where we had to show our hand. We gave chase but didn't catch him. He must have had a hiding spot nearby. Not a shot was fired."

"Well, that's a good start. You'll get Carlo next time. I'm so glad you're okay. I won't bother you anymore, but I'll treat you to a special night out when you're ready. Okay?"

"Sounds great. I'll call you, Ell."

Ellen hung up, relieved that at least her good friend was home and safe.

# Chapter 14

The morning was perfect, bright and beautiful. Brady was ready for a romp and joyfully ran with her to feed and check her cattle.

As Ellen rattled the bucket and called for them, she realized the monster was back. Old Rogue came charging up with the herd. Quickly spreading the cubes, Ellen got behind a large tree. Old Rogue might not be able to stop short enough. When the cows had settled and were eating cubes, Ellen went to check the fence. It was fine. Someone had intentionally unhooked the latch and opened the gate. Who would have done that? For sure, not Old Rogue. Ellen examined the ground for tracks.

*Well, who in the world would do that?* she wondered. *Some trespasser, but why?*

She closed and latched the gate, so there was no danger of her cows getting out of her pasture, and Zack's herd could not come over and mix with hers. She'd leave Old Rogue in with her cows until she had more time or some help. What could it hurt?

*Oh, no! Agnes! Agnes could get into trouble. Old Rogue's offspring could be pretty big, and Agnes didn't need that.*

Agnes was the only one of Ellen's cows that was not pregnant. She would move her to the small pasture on the other side of the barn for now.

After moving Agnes, Ellen went to inspect her garden for insects. Today was not a harvest-and-deliver day. She was glad. She would pickle some beets before going to work on Zack's yard.

When Ellen arrived later in the morning, Zack was just backing out of his drive.

"Can you spare me a minute?" she asked.

"Certainly," he responded, turning off the motor in his truck.

She was close enough to smell his after-shave. The curl that wanted a life of its own, still did. She wanted to....

*Stop it, Ellen,* she instructed herself.

"First, do you want the crepe myrtle trimmed to look like trees or leave them as bushes?" she asked.

"Think I like them as trees best."

"Okay. Next, Old Rogue is back in my pasture. Someone had unlatched the gate and it was open."

"Unlatched the gate?" he seemed concerned.

"Yes, and there were tracks. Large boot tracks. Had to be a man."

"Be careful. Call me if you see anyone you don't know. Immediately okay?"

"Sure"

"As for Old Rogue, he's just that...old. I am trading him for a purebred Limousin bull. Just in case he likes your pasture too." He smiled. "And we'll call him 'Rogue,' as well. 'Young Rogue' or 'Tiny Rogue' maybe, or just 'Tiny.'" He chuckled. "We'll figure it out."

His eyes softened as they swept her completely. What did he mean *we?*

"Please take special care for awhile, all right?"

"Why?"

"Because I wouldn't want anything bad to happen to you, and the wolves are mating now." He smiled and winked, started his truck and drove away.

*What was that supposed to mean? Stay away from Ron? Or actual wolves who would be more aggressive because it was their mating season? No, he means something unusual is about to happen.* She thought. *Something dangerous.*

153

Ellen spent the rest of the day working like a Trojan. She planted all the nursery items she had in stock. She would probably be able to finish up in one more day, but could do nothing else until the plants she ordered arrived.

She bent over to pick up her tools and ripped a seam in her jeans.

*Gracious! That could be embarrassing. All my jeans are really worn. I'll just go into Malden and get some new ones,* she decided.

As she entered the department store in Malden, she noticed a beautiful white peignoir set on a mannequin. After purchasing the jeans she came for, she asked to try her size in the peignoir on display. She loved it. When would she wear it? She'd put it in her hope chest, maybe. Hah! Who cared? She loved it. She bought it.

Returning to her truck, she saw Sandy hurrying back towards the library.

"What's your hurry, girl?" she called out to her.

"Oh, Ell! Hi. I just had lunch with Ron, and I couldn't quit talking. I'm running late."

"Ah, Hah! Is it okay if I take him to dinner soon?"

"It's okay if you're home by nine o'clock. Call me." She laughed and hurried off.

As Ellen reached the end of her drive and turned in, Brady ran to meet her. She let him run loose now, and he was usually within calling range. He was growing really fast and would be a big dog. He already looked formidable—if you didn't know his sweet disposition.

She petted him and told him what a good boy he was. He must already know that, she supposed, since he just trotted away and started chasing grasshoppers.

That afternoon, Ellen received a call that her plant order had arrived at the post office in Malden. Would she come by and pick it up?

"You mean it's too big for my box?" she joked with Jody, whom she knew well.

Jody laughed, "Well, yeah, you'll need your truck, I think."

"How late can I pick it up?"

"I'm here 'til 4:30," Jody replied.

"I'll be there," Ellen said.

Ellen called Ron.

"Would you like to have dinner on my tab at about six this evening?" she asked. We can run over to Amber City and do it up fancier, if you'd like."

"Naw, Malden's food is just as good and not so expensive."

"Yeah, but the atmosphere is better there," she said.

"When you're here, the atmosphere is great," he replied. "And 6 o'clock is fine. I get off at 5 and will be at home if you can pick me up at my place? Do you know where I live?"

"Yep. See you at 6."

Ellen scurried around and picked up the nursery stock just as Jody was ready to lock up.

She had to pick up some items at Wal-Mart and some special make-up and shampoo at her favorite department store. She picked Ron up promptly at 6.

After they were seated and waiting for their food, Ellen asked if there were any news about Bud.

"No, we haven't been able to get any of the guys we arrested to drop a dime on Carlo or anybody else. My guess is they don't know anything."

"I am so worn out and bewildered. I feel I need to do something, but I don't know what."

"What we need is for Lila to give us another time and place," Ron told her.

"She'll probably be out soon. Are the bugs still operational?"

"Yes, I'm sure they are."

"You know, Carlo must really be crazy over Lila to attempt or commit murder for her, don't you think?"

"Well, don't forget Lila thinks she has a $500,000 life insurance policy on Bud. That's a lot of money— even split fifty-fifty." After a bit, Ron remarked, "Oh, by the way, a small grocer with an in-house butcher's shop over in Brighton has admitted to killing Old Seizer. You can file charges if you want, but he was heavily fined. Seems remorseful."

"Did he say why? I'm sure it was the traps."

Ron shrugged his shoulders and shook his head "no."

"I should have turned his traps over to the Sheriff's Department. The old geezer was trapping illegally. How would he feel if someone shot his dog?" She hesitated and continued, "I guess I was wrong to take his traps even though I didn't intend to keep them. I just wanted to talk to him, and I didn't know how to contact him or even who he was. Still wrong. Didn't work either."

"We all make mistakes. At least yours wasn't malicious. Do you want to press charges?"

After short contemplation, Ellen said, "No, I don't think so. Let sleeping dogs lie."

As they enjoyed their dinner, Ellen told Ron of Sandy's admonition to have him home by 9. He chuckled.

"She's a nice girl," he said.

"She's bright, lovely and dependable. She's a great catch and she loves you, you know."

She patted his hand. His smile was relaxed, happy. Ellen suspected he already knew what she had just told him and he liked it.

Ellen did indeed have him home before nine and home herself by the time the clock struck the hour. As she was getting ready for bed, the phone rang.

It was Harry, her ex.

"Hi, Ell, this is Harry. Hope it's not too late to call."

"What can I do for you?" Ellen asked.

"Well, lots of things really, but I won't ask them all."

She said nothing. The silence extended to absurdity.

Finally he said, "I guess Lila has told you that I am indebted to her lover beyond redemption."

"No. I didn't know."

"It was my gambling, and they run a casino down here. Poker... you know how I couldn't leave it alone."

Ellen said nothing.

"I have to make monthly payments, and Lila comes down to collect them. I think he must give her the total amount or she wouldn't come," he continued.

Ellen didn't comment.

"I still have a law practice, but it takes all I can make to pay them off. I'm not gambling now, simply because I have no money to do it with."

"What's the point of all this?" Ellen asked. "If it's money you want, I have none to give you. Mine is all invested. I wouldn't give it to you to pay a gambling debt anyway."

"No, it's not that. First I want to apologize for being a complete idiot. I don't know how I managed to marry someone who could do so many things so well. I regret that I didn't take advantage of the many opportunities I had to love you through him."

"Through him?"

"Jesus Christ," he answered.

"Oh, did we get religion?" she asked.

"Well, when you find yourself on the doorstep to hell and no way out, you take a long look at how you got there." He sounded repentant.

"I'm sorry. But why call me? What does that have to do with me now?"

"I just wanted to let you know that I realize how much I have lost. And I need to give you some information that, maybe, will be of use to you and to me."

*What could that possibly be?* she wondered.

"As you know, Lila has a big mouth. She said they had intended to kill Bud. But he fought back and was getting away. Carlo shot Pedro intending to hit Bud. Bud got away. He was hurt; they don't know how bad. They don't even know if he lived or not. They don't know where he is, but they think he's still alive and that OSBI has him protected. I don't know how they know that. They suspect your neighbor. They were trying to find out for sure, but haven't been able to. Lila thinks they will wipe him out anyway and soon. If Bud is there, they will get him too."

Ellen's heart raced wildly. *Heaven forbid! I have to tell Zack—the sheriff—Ron—everyone has to keep this from happening!*

"They are setting a date and time, and if Lila lets me know what they are, I'll call you back. And no, I'm not really religious. I am grinding an axe of my own, as well. If OSBI gets Carlo and his bunch, I'm off the hook. Maybe, I can still become a halfway decent guy with a chance to pay my own bills."

"Thank you for this information," Ellen said. "I wish you the best and please do call if you find out anything else."

"My head is on the chopping block if they find out I told you."

"I'll not divulge it to anyone but the authorities," she promised. "And I'm sure they will be discreet. This is information they have been waiting for."

She was immediately on the phone to Zack. He sounded sleepy, but was obviously jolted awake with the news she gave him.

"Thanks, a lot, Ell. This is big and it's dangerous. We need to get you some protection as well. I'll call the sheriff and OSBI myself."

She hung up. Confused, she had not even asked if he were the secret agent man, Sid.

The next call was to Ron, and she repeated the same things Harry had told her.

He was excited. "This may all shake out soon. Why don't you stay with Sandy for awhile?"

"Ron! For heaven sakes! I have livestock, pets and a producing garden to look after. I have to stay. I'll hide if I see them coming." She laughed.

"Not funny, Ell. They're extremely dangerous."

"I know," she said seriously. "I'll be careful."

She loved that sweet guy. Sandy was lucky.

Ellen didn't sleep at all, and Brady got to stay inside all night. He found the foot of her bed comfortable, it seemed. He didn't move all night and then stretched lazily when he did wake in the morning.

As tired as she was, she still had to have something to do, so as soon as possible, she went to Zack's and immersed herself in productive labor. The yard was finished and was beautiful; it would be more so as time went by. She hoped he'd be pleased.

She slept soundly that night, and so did Brady at the end of her bed.

Ellen woke the next morning realizing she had forgotten to ask Sandy why she had underlined Zack's initials on the printout of his history. She took the paper out of her desk drawer and studied it to see if it told her anything about his connection to OSBI. She had not figured out anything and decided nothing was there when Lila knocked on the door.

Leaving the information on her desk, she went to see who was there. Lila came in, critical as ever.

"Why do you keep that scary looking mutt,

anyway? He looks like he could whip a bear."

"I hope he can, but that he never has to," Ellen commented.

Lila was soon drinking and talking. Ellen left her in the den to put out food for Old Yowler and Miss Muffy. When she returned, Lila was sitting at her desk staring at the printout Sandy had given Ellen about Zack.

She had written something on it and with a big laugh, she said, "Well, well! At last!"

She jumped up, saying she really had to run and left. Her glass with most of her last drink was setting on the desk. What had she seen that had caused her to leave in such a hurry? She never left any booze behind. What had Ellen missed?

Ellen looked again at the printout. The underlined initials <u>D</u>aniel <u>I</u>saac <u>C</u>unningham were reversed. They were CID or Sid.

*Oh, God! How did I miss it? It is true! And now they know for sure! They had intended to kill him because they had suspected he was Sid, the agent who was trying to run Carlo and his gang out of the country. They will surely do so now that they have what appears to be proof.*

Ellen ran to the phone and called Zack immediately.

When he answered, she said, "They know! They know for sure now, and it's my fault. I had a printout of your history on my desk with your full name. Lila figured out your initials backward spell Cid or Sid. I'm so sorry. She left in a hurry. Oh God! I'm sorry!"

"They would have found out anyway. Don't worry. We'll be ready. Ell, go stay with Sandy or get a motel or something, but be safe. Promise me. They are extremely dangerous, and they'll do anything to keep their drug operation here. They won't bother you unless they get us first is my guess. But be safe. Promise me."

"I promise. I'll do my best to stay out of harm's way."

He hung up.

How to be safe? Exactly what should she do? Who knew when they would come? She would do her chores as she tried to determine exactly how to best avoid danger from the cartel hoods.

Brady followed Ellen. She fed and counted her livestock. Brady was off and running—over the hill and out of sight. She heard him bark. It became an angry expression of get-out-you-don't-belong barking and growling. A shot rang out.

"Oh, God! Please no!" She screamed and ran in the direction of the shot.

She remembered Seizer and what had happened to him. Not this precious puppy too! She had to cross the creek. She jumped into the water, boots and all. About halfway across, Brady met her. He was so glad to see her he almost knocked her down.

*Discretion is the better part of valor!* She was half-crying and half-laughing from relief. *Thank God, Brady knew when it was time to run.*

She called him and they both hurried to the house. Was this it then? Were they here already? She locked Brady in the utility and went outside to the highest point around her house and saw nothing. What should she do? She felt she should at least feed Agnes. With her bucket of cubes, she went cautiously to the cattle pen. Agnes appreciated her supper.

# Chapter Fifteen

As Ellen, carrying her bucket, was almost back to the house, Lila stepped into view.

"Well, well, sweet little Ell. I want to introduce my very good friend, Carlo."

Carlo was not a tall man nor was he good-looking. In fact, he was downright ugly.

*No wonder Lila wanted extra dinner dates!*

He grinned like a robot. There was no expression in his eyes. They were cold, hard, calculating. *A snake! Yeah. That's what he was. Too late to run.* Ellen shivered.

She *remembered Zack and Ron saying, "These are dangerous people."* She believed it.

Where's your brother?" he demanded.

"I don't know. If you can tell me anything about him, I would really appreciate it."

What else could she say? His laugh was short and brittle. He pulled out a gun from under his armpit. Ellen gasped.

Lila laughed. "Better tell him, sweetie. He always wins."

*Maybe not always,* Ellen thought. *He has you, and I don't think that's a winner's prize.*

"Git inside. We'll see if he's here." Carlo shoved her towards the house.

Almost without a sound, Ron appeared from behind the azaleas, a gun in his hand. Still Carlo heard him. He turned and took aim. Ellen slammed her bucket across his arm with all her strength. The gun discharged into the air. Carlo cursed. His gun flew under the fence.

Lila screamed, "Carlo, here!"

162

She somehow had a gun in her hand. She threw it to Rodriguez. It was too late. A deafening roar shattered the surroundings. Ron's bullet found its target. Carlo was dead before he hit the ground.

"Carlo, Carlo," Lila screamed hideously. "You have killed him, you bastard."

Some grief, some anger and some determination were all expressed throughout her shrieking tirade. Several words were clearly discernible and often repeated. Notably, "I'll kill you! I'll kill you! I'll kill you all!"

She cursed them all: Bud, Ron and Ellen. She used language unconscionably disgusting. She cursed Jen and Bud's baby and said it would die.

"You can't keep me from getting what I want by using that bastard baby! We'll kill him too!" she screamed. "Ron, you f...ing SOB, you want that bitch, Ellen. You killed my Carlo, now we'll kill her! I'll still get all she's got."

As she threatened and flailed her arms about, a small gold cigarette case fell from her pocket. She bent to pick it up. As she straightened, another roar filled the air. She fell slowly, headlong into a flowerbed of petunias. Lila stopped screeching. A gurgle came from her throat. Ron had shot her. Fatally.

Ellen was stunned. What had just happened? Lila was just reaching for her fallen cigarette case. Ron must have thought she was going for the gun she had thrown to Carlo, the gun that had fallen at Ellen's feet? Or was he so incensed by the filthiness of Lila's threats that he just did her in? Ellen had wanted to choke the breath out of Lila herself.

Had Ron believed Lila might carry out her threats? If she didn't, would some of Rodriguez's vengeful assassins do so? Especially if she encouraged them?

Ellen heard sounds of approaching officers. She

wondered what penalties Ron would have to pay.

Should he have to pay or even be questioned about his shooting of Lila? Should he be investigated, spend the rest of his life viewed with suspicion of being unworthy of his badge? If Lila could have, she would have killed them all. She had her cohorts beat up Bud and maybe even had killed him. And they had killed one of their own and buried him in her pasture. There was proof of it all. No! By all that was holy, no! Ron should not be penalized.

Ellen quickly kicked Lila's fallen gun towards her body. It landed about a foot in front of where she had fallen. Ellen then fell to her knees, picking up and pocketing the small gold cigarette case.

Officers were all around them before she could rise. She stayed on her knees, covered her face and started weeping.

"She was going to kill me! She was going to kill me!" she cried.

After several minutes, when Ellen seemingly had herself under control, Sheriff Hewitt questioned her about what had happened.

Ellen told him Rodriguez had tried to shoot Ron. Ellen knocked the gun away with her bucket, but Lila threw Rodriguez another gun. Ron had managed to shoot Carlo before he could aim. The gun fell to the ground, and Lila went for it, screaming she would kill them all.

"Yeah, we heard a lot of that screeching," he said.

"She was going to kill me, but Ron shot her first." Ellen was again crying softly.

"We will need you to come in tomorrow to sign a statement," Sheriff Hewitt gravely replied .

"Yes, of course," Ellen agreed, wiping the tears from her cheeks.

The sheriff took Ron's gun as a matter of course.

Carlo's gun was found on the other side of the fence. Ron was staring at Ellen in wide-eyed amazement. Her lips formed a kiss for him and then a gentle half-smile. Ron's pursed lips subtlety displayed the bare hint of a smile as he gave her a slight wag of his head from side to side. His eyes spoke of thankfulness and gratitude. They told her he thought she was one hell of a woman. He turned to follow the sheriff. Who could prove what flashed through a man's mind in a moment of extreme duress. Ellen couldn't be sure. Maybe Ron wasn't even sure himself. But no one could deny that justice had been served.

Yells and curses punctuated by sharp reports of gunfire filled the air. An occasional siren blast was heard, as officers of the law chased unyielding suspects with their cruisers. SWAT team members escorted others, handcuffed and resisting, to be locked in squad cars.

After all the commotion had settled and the scene had been thoroughly investigated, Ellen still sat on the upturned bucket she had used to knock the gun from Carlo's hand. Almost everyone else had left or was leaving. She was still in shock, too numb or too tired to move.

She heard a soft, feminine voice behind her. Turning, she was surprised to see Jennifer walking towards her.

"Oh, Lord, Jen, you shouldn't be here! It was so dangerous, so brutal, so…unholy." Ellen found tears on her cheeks again.

Jennifer, too, was crying softly. "Yes, but thank God it's all over now. All of it. We don't have to hide anymore."

She hugged Ellen. Ellen wondered what she meant. *Who was hiding? Bud?*

"I have something to tell you that you will want to

hear, but it will make you angry as well. Oh, God, Ell. I'm so sorry we had to do what we did, but it seemed the best way to protect us all."

"What? What are you talking about?" Ellen exclaimed, puzzled.

"This will come as a shock, so why don't we go into the house and sit while I tell you the whole story?"

Ellen went into the kitchen and made a pot of coffee. Who could sleep anyway? Brady was scratching at the utility room door. Thinking it was now safe to do so, Ellen let him outside. When the coffee was ready, Ellen and Jennifer went into the den. Jennifer nervously began to explain.

"As you now know, Lila was behind the plot to kill Bud and get his insurance money, plus half of your business. Well, at first she was. But we were afraid if she killed Bud, she would then kill me—because of the baby. And if she had Bud's share of your business, she would be your partner. Your contract with Bud has a "rights of survivorship" clause, meaning if one person dies, the other partner gets everything. They would have killed you too. She would have it all."

Jennifer stopped and wiped her cheeks. She continued, "Ell, I know it must seem stupid to you, but after weighing the pros and cons, everyone—even OSBI—agreed it was the best plan. Speaking of OSBI, you know that Zack is in charge of the undercover unit there, don't you?"

"Yes, I finally figured that out."

"The more people who knew about Bud, the more there would be who had to be protected. And that's a tough job. Just protecting one is an enormous responsibility. Plus, we needed you to act just as you did. So hurt, so involved in trying to find Bud that those watching you would be convinced that you had no clue where he was. And, of course, you didn't. We kept that secret well." Jennifer was crying again. "Please, Ell, forgive us. I know how much it hurt, but we did the best we could to keep us all safe. These people were extremely dangerous."

Ellen was stunned. Was Jennifer saying they had known all along where Bud was? And they didn't tell her? They let her rack her brain, cry her heart out and try every trick she could think of—even considering torture—to make Lila give up information?

Someone opened the door behind her. As Ellen turned and recognized who stood there on crutches, she screamed, stood and wavered, but only for a brief second.

Sobbing she ran to Bud, crying, "Oh Lord! Oh, Lord! I thought I'd never see you again.

Bud was crying too. He had dropped one of his crutches and was leaning against the wall for support. Putting one arm around her, he said, "Sis, I'm so sorry to have hurt you that way, but it seemed best for us all…you too. I wanted with all my heart to tell you—and almost did a time or two. But all those who were behind it are now dead or in custody. So maybe we can patch it all together and move on. We still have each other."

Ellen was still crying and holding onto Bud. She wouldn't let go.

Finally, he said, "You better let me sit down before you have to pick me up off the floor."

Ellen immediately helped him to a chair.

"Where have you been all this time?" She finally asked.

"Zack's. Zack was protecting us both. He's really a great guy."

"Yeah. A mighty fine neighbor, I guess." Of course it had to be Zack. Why had she been so blind and not seen it sooner? She had begun to have suspicions but never thought Bud would be in the house next door.

"But...but how did you end up in Zack's house?"

"I was hurt and hurt bad...but I had to get away. So even with a broken leg, cracked ribs and a concussion, plus a bloody nose, I managed to stumble, fall or roll to get outside. They were on my tail pretty fast after they absorbed the shock of my falling at the right time, causing Carlo to hit Pedro instead. But they heard Zack's truck coming and opted to get away instead of do me in. Zack saw me floundering around trying to get up and stopped to help. He rushed me to the hospital."

"And I was upset because he was driving so fast down the road." Ellen expressed self-deprecation, shaking her head with tears brightening her eyes.

"Lila had bragged about her Carlo, 'the king of the underworld.' When I told Zack, he knew immediately who was involved. OSBI took a look at all the evidence and decided I needed protection and maybe so did you and Jennifer. We all agreed to do it the way we did...all except you, Ell. We used you, I guess, but we were also trying to protect you and all of us." He reached out and squeezed her hand.

"Did Zack buy out here just to be close and watch the cartel guys?"

"No, I don't think so. He's just a love-the-country kind of a guy. He liked what he found and bought it. Wonderful coincidence, huh?"

"Yes, is he okay? After tonight? Do you know?" Anxiety caused Ellen to lean forward in her chair, dreading an answer.

"Yeah, he was in the thick of it tonight. This was a big dealer that OSBI had been trying to catch for a long while. Zack took some of the major guys to Oklahoma City and will make his reports. He wouldn't leave until he knew you and Ron were okay. But, yeah, he's alright. He'll probably be back tomorrow."

"Oh, by the way, Bud, did you change your insurance policy and make Jennifer the beneficiary?"

"Yeah, I did. And the Sheriff gave me an escort to Globe Life to do it," he laughed.

"That must've been the little convoy I met going down the road the other day."

It dawned on Ellen suddenly that everything was being heard through the "bug" under her table. She walked over, bent down and said loudly, "You guys are a bunch of eavesdroppers or voyeurs or something. But as Hillary has said, 'it takes a village.' And we are so glad you guys are a part of our village. But whatever you are, we love you bunches." Then she jerked the bug from its mountings.

Bud accepted a cup of coffee, and Ellen and Jennifer had refills. Ellen made sandwiches, and they discussed how Sheriff Hewitt's men, OSBI and the SWAT teams were so well-coordinated and all there at just the right time.

"Harry was a critical asset when he told Ellen that Carlo and his men were intending to kill Zack. And when Lila found out for sure Zack was "Sid," law enforcement figured it was show time. So they were ready and waiting."

Ellen apologized for thinking Jennifer was betraying Bud with Zack.

"I should have known better, well..., actually, I did know better, but you guys seemed so...well...together. I lost my faith, I guess," she said. "I'm sorry."

Jennifer accepted the apology graciously. "We needed you to believe it though we were as miserable about it as you were. It was a horrible thing to do to you, but you handled it well."

Ellen didn't think so.

Soon Bud said, "Ell, honey, we all need some rest so we'll go now and see you tomorrow. Will you be alright or would you like to come home with us?"

It had been an exhausting day, and Jennifer looked haggard. Bud showed signs of fatigue as well, but his concern was obviously for Jennifer and his unborn child.

Ellen declined. "I am so tired and confused, and I ran through the creek so I'm dirty as a pig. I guess I'll soak in the tub, then get some sleep. Maybe I'll just sleep in the tub," she remarked.

Bud chuckled. Everyone hugged each other again. Tears filled Ellen's eyes and trickled down her checks.

"I love you guys so much. Bud, please don't get lost again."

"We love you too, Ell. Please forgive us."

"Of course," she said. But it hurt. She would have to work her way through that. Surely they could have told her.

Bud was an eyewitness that Carlo had killed Pedro and that Lila was an accomplice. They could have arrested them months ago. But OSBI had wanted to shut down Carlo completely, stop the gun running and drug trafficking altogether. They had hoped to eliminate any possible retaliatory threat to any of them. Zack had been trying to do that for a long time. He had asked and received Bud's and Jennifer's cooperation.

But it still hurt. True, it was a good cause, but they had used her. She was a significant player in the scheme, and they had not consulted her. It felt as though they couldn't trust her. She could have kept their secret. Then she thought of Lila's discovery. Lila had learned that Zack was Sid through Ellen's scribblings of Zack's initials. Maybe it was safer to have done it their way, but it hurt nonetheless.

Ellen was so tired she just fed her cats and Brady and went straight to her bath. Questions and answers were whirling around in her head trying to match up with each other.

*Will I ever sort it all out? And come to terms with it?* She would try.

She soaked in the tub for a while and then washed her hair in a wonderful-smelling shampoo. It made her hair soft and shiny with a slight curl that caressed her checks and neck. She brushed it well and left it down—to fall softly about her face.

She felt somewhat relaxed after her bath, but knew she could not sleep. She decided to be nice to herself, so she poured a glass of her favorite wine, Barringer's White Zinfandel, and went into the bedroom to try on her new peignoir set. The negligee was a bit sheerer than she usually wore, but it was wonderfully soft and so beautiful that Ellen hadn't been able to resist it.

*I must have been having a fanciful dream or delusions when I bought this,* she thought.

She sat down with her White Zinfandel and let her mind wander.

So Zack was in charge of the undercover OSBI unit in Oklahoma City. He really was a cool character. She would find it difficult to forgive him though. He had kept her in misery for months. She was glad she had finished his yard. She wouldn't have to be near him anymore. At least for a long while. Then maybe they could be good friends, if she could keep her emotions under control. She wondered what he meant when he said he had something to discuss with her. Remembering the look in his eyes, she thought it was a reflection of the longing in her heart. What if...?

Ellen was astonished at her own misconceived perception about the relationship between Zack and Jennifer. Her failed marriage had left her with a skewed notion that men were just naturally philanderers. She had readily accepted the worst about Zack. She believed Zack had seduced Jennifer at her most vulnerable time…pregnant and alone. Her judgment had been totally wrong, based on that false premise. But of course, everyone had worked to make her believe there was an affair.

Brady gave a sharp bark.

*Must be a 'possum,* she thought.

But, when he kept barking, she went to check it out.

A car was pulling up to her door. She stepped into the shadows, not knowing whom to expect.

Zack stepped out of the car and said, "Ell?"

He had seen her before she slipped behind the corner of the porch. What was he doing here? Probably looking for Bud. She was feeling a mix of emotions: joy that he was not attached to Jennifer, relief he was not hurt, love in abundance—but anger also. How could he care for her at all and let her suffer the way he had. He surely knew how much it had hurt.

She stepped out of the shadows.

"Ell, please talk to me. Let me explain. Please forgive me."

She couldn't believe he would have the audacity to ask for her forgiveness. She was angry enough to strike him. Tears stung her eyes, confusion engulfed her as she turned to flee. He was there somehow in front of her. Reaching out, his arms encircled her.

She stopped short, exasperated and hissed, "How dare you expect me to forgive such a hurtful thing as you have perpetrated?" But his arms closed around her and gently drew her into a wonderfully safe and comforting place that overwhelmed her senses.

"It had to be done that way, Ell. Please give me a chance to tell you everything."

In spite of her desire to stay in his arms, close to his very core, she struggled to escape. Thoughts of long past betrayals fleetingly spread through her mind, thoughts of sleepless nights and broken promises, caused her to break free of his embrace.

Running towards her house, she cried, "Don't ever speak to me again!"

She tried to slam the door, but he caught it…and her. More forcefully than before, his arms embraced her. "Ell, please wait," he begged.

Something she longed for…found in the tone of his voice…spoke to her heart, and she hesitated.

He drew her close. His lips touching her forehead, moving down her cheeks were soon tenderly on her mouth. His hands moved upward, across her shoulders and softly brushing the back of her neck, threaded themselves into her hair.

Her body relaxed as he pleadingly whispered, "Please, Ell, don't throw this away without at least hearing me out."

She ran her fingers through her hair and pushed it back. But it had a mind of its own and fell softly about her face and neck. He buried his face in it with a groan. His mouth caressed her throat, kissed beneath her ear. His tongue teased the corner of her mouth. His hands began to explore on their own. A low sob escaped her as they found their way to places she had longed for him to touch, but never dared to hope for. Ellen was completely overwhelmed. She had wanted him so desperately and now being in his arms, knowing he wanted her too, was almost too much for her to control.

Huskily, he whispered, "You gotta love me too," he pleaded. "And you do. You do love me too, don't you?"

Unable to speak, her arms went around his neck. There was relief in his voice when he finally spoke.

"I hoped it was so…because I have to have you, obstinate though you are. Please say you are mine and will be forever."

He told her so much with so few words. He loved her. He had hoped for that closeness as she had. He knew by her responses that she loved him too. He thought her obstinate, maybe even pushy, but he wanted her anyway. And perhaps that "forever" he had mentioned was a proposal.

She was still too speechless to verbally validate his thoughts. Here was her long-wished for partner, though she would hardly have acknowledged that to herself. She felt the love and strength in him and readily gave in to it, aching to be a part of it—wanting to give and to receive, knowing he would always be that someone special in her life. Here was a man she could respect—a man strong enough to be his own person and still give of himself to another. She knew he would love and support her always. And she knew in her heart that she would still be her own person, independent and creative. She was intimately and inextricably bound to this man who filled her heart to overflowing with an exquisite longing for that love and closeness marriage was intended to be.

What differences they might have about the handling of information she had desperately needed about Bud would have to be sorted out. Regardless of what happened, she knew she had to have Zack too, and she was not about to walk away from this. Somehow, though, she couldn't reveal her vulnerability. He would possess her completely if she did.

Brushing the tears from her cheeks and tossing her head somewhat defiantly, she cleared her throat and said, "Well, let's just keep one thing straight. Keep your old rogue of a bull out of my pasture. At least, until my cows invite him over. Okay?"

He chuckled. Putting his hands on her bottom, he pulled her snug up against him. and covered her mouth once more with his own. Her arms went around him, unable to hold him close enough. The kiss was long and tender, causing her to tremble with the need of him.

When he released her, his hand caressed her cheek and as he cleared his throat and spoke, the timbre of his voice and the gentleness of his touch told her the moment had moved him as well.

"I'll do my dead level best, sweetheart. If you will make sure those engraved invitations are for Rogue alone. But if my pastures are your pastures, are invitations really necessary? Or even fences? Is there such a thing as right of trespass?"

He bent, swept her up and carried her into the dimly lit den. "Are the listening devices still operational?" he asked.

"No. I unplugged them."

"Good!" As he set her down, he studied her from head to toe. Gently pulling her close, he whispered, "You are so beautiful." Taking her face in both his hands, he said, "Ellie, it was so hard not to reach for you when I wanted you so much. It was almost more than I could handle. He stopped talking and kissed her all over the face: on her forehead, her neck, under her ear, even her eyelids. His tongue teased the corners of her mouth. With a groan he gathered her up close and softly asked, "You do love me, don't you? Please tell me you do."

"I do love you, my darling, rogue, with all my heart and soul. Only you teased, then backed away. I thought it was because you had a prior commitment with Jen. I thought I would die from the want of you."

"I didn't mean to tease, my love. I just got carried away before I remembered I had to leave you alone. Thank God that's all over. We belong together, sweetheart. His hands gently moved the lace fabric from her shoulders and, as it fell softly to the floor, his breath caught sharply, "Oh God, Ellie." His voice was husky; his hands moved over the satiny smoothness of her skin to caress the small of her back. He kissed her tenderly on the mouth.

*Had she died and gone to heaven?* She could hardly breathe. Why ask all those questions? Didn't he know she wanted him as much as he wanted her? Her arms went around his neck. As he bent, she stood on tiptoe and gently pressed his cheek against her naked bosom. His mouth found something else to tease.

Softly, he whispered, "Could this be a rogue invitation? Or am I about to trespass?"

"If my pastures are your pastures, there can be no trespass." She snuggled close and pleaded, "Just please don't ever jump any fences and graze anyone else's pastures."

He groaned. "Not a chance in hell," he muttered close to her ear as he gathered her up and carried her towards the bedroom and the promise of a future filled with green pastures without fences and the right of trespass.

# Right of Trespass

www.ingramcontent.com/pod-product-compliance
Lightning Source LLC
Chambersburg PA
CBHW060222180626
46813CB00007B/2932